A Slight Miscalculation

...As Jett turned away, the creature pursued him with blinding speed and grabbed him in its tentacles. It pulled him up toward its checkerboard chest plate. The center opened and an octopus like beak emerged. Everything went black...

THE TINKER & THE FOLD

Part I - Problem with Solaris 3

By Evan & Scott Gordon

Laguna Lantern Publishing Company

Published by:
Laguna Lantern Publishing Company
Laguna Niguel, CA 92677

USA * Canada * UK * Australia * India
China * Mexico * EU * South Africa

First published in the United States of America
by Laguna Lantern Publishing Company.

Laguna Lantern Publishing Co. ISBN 978-0-9963574-3-2

Printed in the United Stated of America

Acknowledgments

Thank you to Dennis & Nancy Duitch, Robert Hoyt, Ann Bryson, and Natalie Pearl for agreeing to read early drafts of this book. Their contributions to our project were very insightful and provided much clarity to both the characters' voices and overall story. We'd also like to thank Chelyn Briand and Eddie Oddo Jr. for being among the early Kindle downloaders of this book who alerted us to several 'editing opportunities' important to the final print version. Thanks all of you for your guidance and inspiration.

- Evan and Scott Gordon, May 2015

*"Life may exist in yonder dark, but it will
not wear the shape of man."*

- Loren Eisley 1957

Chapter 1
Spooky Action

Jett stopped typing and placed his tablet on his desk. He looked up at the clock.

"Two-thirty," he moaned. It would be another half-hour before school let out and he'd be able to go home and finish his project for the science fair.

"Mr. Javelin, is there something you'd like to share with the rest of the class?" Mrs. Aspen fussed.

"Huh?" Jett said caught unawares.

"That's fifteen minutes after class for not paying attention," she remarked.

"Ugh," Jett moaned, "This sucks..."

"Excuse me, Mr. Javelin?"

"Um, yes, Ma'am, after class. Looking forward to it. Good times, great memories."

The classed laughed.

"That's enough! Finish your work," Mrs. Aspen ordered sternly.

Heads went down and fingers tapped furiously.

Recently, things hadn't been easy for Jett at school. Ever since Halloween, after Jett permanently dyed his hair blue in a freak costume mishap, Mrs. Aspen had been unusually cross with him. His Nightcrawler costume was a huge hit, but his permanent blue hair was a massive price to pay for a sugar high and some cheap no-name candy.

Strangely, the new look had grown on Jett and his family, that is everyone except for his twin brother Jack.

"Hey, Mr. Ty-D-Bol," Jack would tease, "there's a ring

in my toilet. I just need your head for a second."

But Jett was done thinking about his stupid brother. He had far more pressing matters to deal with. Ever since he had stumbled upon his mother's papers on Quantum Exchange, his mind had been riveted by possibility.

Today was the day Jett planned to set his mother's theories into motion. What was another few minutes in school after all? He was about to change the world. Elon Musk and Steve Jobs would have nothing on him. His invention would trump them all.

"Jett, stop day dreaming," Mrs. Aspen snapped him to attention, "It's a quarter after three. I thought you were in a hurry to get home."

"I'm, um, sorry, I must have lost track of time. See you tomorrow," Jett called out as he quickly gathered his things and raced out the door to the jingling of his father's old army dog tags.

When Jett arrived home, he hurried upstairs to his bedroom. He needed to tinker with his Quantum Swapper so it would be ready for the trial phase. He tossed his backpack onto his bed and hurried to his cluttered workbench.

He required some special tools:

1. Blowtorch
2. High intensity laser pen (his most recent invention)
3. Fine screwdriver set
4. Wire crimper
5. E.M.P. grenade (because electro-magnetic pulses come in handy in the event one needs to disable electronic devices – say an army of murderous robots)
6. iTouch and his *patent pending* 'Swapper App'

7. 3D printer (in the event he needed to fabricate replacement parts)

Cords were strewn across the bedroom floor in elaborate patterns. They ran up and down the hallway outside his room, and thirstily sucked electricity wherever they could find it.

"I hope I don't blow out the breakers again. Dad can be *sensitive* about these sorts of things," he muttered.

Jett made several adjustments to the machine, checked its voltage and current, used his laser pen to trim off an untidy piece of plastic. When he was satisfied that everything was in order, he pressed the record button on his tripod-mounted iPad and began his demonstration.

"Hello, my name is Jett Joseph Javelin Jr., and I'm transmitting from San Jose, California. I'm about to demonstrate my latest invention: The Quantum Swapper. I'm going to beam Yoda here," Jett motioned to a Lego character, "from his perch atop the Quantum Swapper into that X-Wing fighter over there," Jett said expertly, "utilizing the theory of quantum exchange."

"Today is Friday November 18th, 2028. The time is 4:47 pm. This will mark the human race's first demonstration of teleportation," Jett finished.

He turned his back to the camera and entered a series of numbers into his iPhone. The Quantum Swapper emitted a low hum, and in a flash of light, Yoda was seated comfortably in the nearby spacecraft.

"Oh my God!" Jett cried, "It worked! It actually worked! See that, world! My Quantum Swapper worked!"

Chapter 2
The Fold's Mandate

The Eelshakians never saw it coming. The same was true of every solar system that had been neutralized since The Great White Light first appeared to the Aaptuuan Council at the dawn of the age of The Ten Laws. Ignorant of the universe beyond the bounds of their own solar systems, the aggressive races believed they were the supreme species.

The Eelshakians were a particularly brutal example of this. After they mastered interplanetary travel, the Eelshakians rained terror and destruction down upon all the planets in their solar system.

As they murdered and plundered, the Eelshakians every action was meticulously recorded; every species they exterminated catalogued; every planet they colonized noted.

For the rules of galactic peace are simple: intelligent races are granted freewill and can do as they please, for better or worse, within the boundaries of their home systems. However, any technological advance that extends their influence beyond their home system triggers a review by the High Council on Aaptuu 4.

If the race in question abides by the tenants of The Ten Laws, a delegation is sent from the Aaptuuan System to extend an invitation to join The Fold. But, if a race is considered dangerous, hostile, or a threat to galactic peace, and *beyond* redemption, it is neutralized: lights out. For the Eelshakians, whose brutal hostility toward other species was well documented, neutralization was the only option.

Le-Wa sat at the control console of his Aaptuuan scout

ship. He recalled the day 7,500 Eelshakian years earlier when he and Chi-Col brought The Ten Simple Laws to this species in the form of two stone tablets. It was long before the Eelshakians had developed interstellar space travel. Le-Wa felt a deep sadness as he went about his tasks. His companion, Chi-Col, empathized. Both had endured this many times before as neutralizations were a brutal affair, but the Eelshakians' black hole generator now posed the greatest threat to galactic peace that the Aaptuuans had observed in nearly a hundred thousand years.

Outside their craft, the Eelshakian civilization buzzed with activity. Large cylindrical transports laden with goods traveled between Eelshaks 3 and 4. These were accompanied by heavily armed Eelshakian Mange"e Class battle cruisers and various frigates and smaller craft.

Eelshak 5 had declared its independence from the Empire and the Ruling Class on Eelshak 4 had developed a secret weapon intended to bring Eelshak 5 and its rebellious merchant class back in line, and more importantly, ensure the continued flow of precious minerals, commodities, and taxes.

"War," Le-Wa thought, "creates such a noise in the Universe. The cries of the dead ring out through the dark matter. So much death and dying. The Eelshakians' biological impulses override logic."

Le-Wa was well acquainted with the voluminous research chronicling the rise and fall of civilizations. The Eelshakians were simply the latest example of a species whose technological prowess had surpassed its ability to use it responsibly.

As the two went about their tasks, a group of Eelshak 5

battle cruisers appeared in the distance and fired upon the cargo convoy. Explosions outside cast shadows about the ship's bridge. Le-Wa and Chi-Col hardly noticed. They went about their business with the cool precision of master watch makers.

"I am detecting unusual activity on the gravity scanner," Le-Wa observed, "The readings are emanating from Eelshak 4 and increasing in strength."

"Confirmed," Chi-Col replied with concern, "It appears that the black hole generator has been activated."

"Odd that they would activate it on their home world."

"Unless, its activation is accidental…"

"The black hole is growing at 1000 cubic meters per second and accelerating," Le-Wa calculated, "gravitational influence on Eelshak 4's two moons is confirmed."

"The moons are accelerating toward Eelshak 4. The larger moon will impact first. The capital city of Ookchorii has been consumed along with 1,000 cubic kilometers of the planet itself. Radio messages from Eelshak 4 are alerting the fleet to the danger," Chi-Col reported.

"It is too late for them, the Eelshakians' primitive propulsion systems will provide insufficient boost to achieve escape velocity from the black hole's gravitation pull."

"Send a report to Aaptuu 4 that the Eelshakians have activated their black hole device and that we are withdrawing from the system without having completed our mission," Le-Wa said, "We will continue to observe the demise of this system from a safe distance away."

"Message transmitted. The black hole is now growing at 10,000 cubic meters per second and accelerating," Chi-Col reported.

The Aaptuuans watched Eelshak 4's second moon collapse into the black hole followed by hundreds of space stations, cruisers, and assorted craft.

"Systems are measuring a strong gravitation influence on Eelshak 3 and the asteroid belt."

"Black hole growth accelerating," Chi-Col warned, "our ship is now affected by the gravitational pull. We need to withdraw further. Eelshak 3 and 5 are now moving toward the anomaly."

"Eelshak 3 to reach the Event Horizon in 10, 9, 8, 7, 6, 5, 4, 3, 2, 1... Event Horizon breached," Le-Wa announced as Eelshak 3 stretched like a deflated rubber balloon into a thin blue and green band before disappearing into the singularity. It was followed by another mass of ships and transports futilely trying to escape.

Eelshak's star and its inner and outer planets, as well as, various asteroids, moons, comets, and other debris converged on the black hole.

"Eelshak 5 approaching Event Horizon in 10, 9, 8, 7, 6, 5, 4, 3, 2, 1... Event Horizon breached," Le-Wa confirmed as the medium sized planet was stretched into an infinitely thin strand spanning millions of kilometers. As with the other two inhabited planets, the myriad ships attempting escape were stretched out and sucked into the black hole in rapid succession.

"Scanning solar system for remaining life forms."

"I am taking us out to a safe distance," Le-Wa replied, "When the system's sun hits the black hole it will mark the end."

The Eelshakian Sun became elongated as it approached

the black hole. It spewed flares and violently ejected plasma in all directions. An eerily beautiful halo engulfed the star. One side of it stretched to a fine point. It looked like a giant orange ice cream cone melting into fiery oblivion.

And with that, the star once known as Eelshak became a long thin flame and was snuffed out forever.

"Star charts have been updated to reflect the loss of the Eelshak system," the ship's computer chirped.

"Scanning the void for space craft and life forms," Le-Wa said, "There are several probes and satellites that have escaped the anomaly. One of the probes appears to have a faint life form aboard. Setting course to intercept."

"The life form is Eelshakia Suprema," Chi-Col announced with surprise, "We do not have any records of piloted craft this far out."

"Well, since it has no home to return to, and it is the last of its kind, it will come with us to Aaptuu 4," Le-Wa replied, "Perhaps it can be rehabilitated."

Upon reaching the Eelshakian craft, Chi-Col carefully guided a probe alongside it and pierced its hull.

"Ready to board," Chi-Col said, "You stay here and monitor the subject's activity and be prepared to neutralize the subject in the event it is armed."

Chi-Col, donning a white metallic space suit, crossed the delicate silver tube through the frigid emptiness of space to retrieve the very last living organism to ever call Eelshak home.

Chapter 3
The Mission for Solaris 3

Hazbog's vision slowly came into focus. As it did, he realized that he was no longer in his hibernation tube. Hazbog wondered where he was; who had found him; and what they might do with him now.

Hazbog found himself in an empty white room. A room with no edges, no windows, or doors. It lacked any definition. It was at once confined and infinite. It was terrifying.

"I am Hazbog," he bellowed, "I am the Commander of the Fifth Navy of Ookchorii. You will show yourself."

Hazbog waited a few moments before he impatiently repeated himself.

"Show yourself!"

Still nothing. Worse, the very sound of his voice was instantly absorbed by the room and muted. It was like shouting into a pillow.

"Show yourself!" Hazbog ordered again.

An outline of a door appeared in front of him. As it opened, he was blinded by a piercing white light.

"One known as Hazbog," a soothing voice echoed, "You are the last of your kind, the last of your solar system. We found you drifting about in the endless darkness."

"Who are you?"

"We are the Keepers of The Ten Laws."

Hazbog thought on this for a moment. The Ten Laws were an old myth from long ago.

"What is this trick you play on me?" he asked. "I am in no mood for children's stories."

"You believe them to be myths," the voice instructed, "but we assure you - they are quite real."

"Real?" Hazbog scoffed, "Real foolish! We gave them up long ago. They are only fairy tales, scary stories we tell the young ones."

"They are not fairy tales."

"How could that be? Who are you?"

"One called Hazbog. You are the very last survivor of your species and the last of all the species that once inhabited your solar system. We regret to inform you that your species exterminated itself and, in fact, all life in your system."

"Impossible," Hazbog said with conviction, "We Ookchorri are preparing to conquer new systems. That's why I was sent on my mission. What such Armageddon could have befallen my people? Stop your trickery at once or..."

"Or what?" the calm voice replied. "You have no idea where you are or who we are or how long we have been watching."

"Watching who, me?"

"Watching your system."

"So why do you harass me?" Hazbog demanded.

"We do not harass. You will return with us to Aaptuu 4 since you have no planet of your own to return to."

"You say the Ookchorii are extinct. What happened?"

"Your species, known as Eelshakia Suprema by The Fold, entered into civil war," the voice began, "Your scientists developed a weapon that was beyond their technical capabilities and your military lost control of it. The device, a black hole generator, consumed your entire system. You survive only because your vessel was beyond the gravitational

10

reach of the black hole."

"What will you do with me?"

"You will be provided with accommodations on our home world. There you will live out the remainder of your brief life."

"Brief life!" Hazbog protested, "I'm only 250 years old. I still have more than half my life left. Your accommodations are no better than a prison cell."

"It will be what you make of it," the voice replied.

Hazbog stared blankly with confusion. Who were these beings? Was what they were telling him true? Where were they taking him? How might he escape?

"Your questions will be answered," the voice informed him, "and you can forget about escape."

"You can read my thoughts?" Hazbog asked.

"Yes, every one of them. We have told you the truth, but you are not yet ready to accept it."

Hazbog pondered this question. Where would he go? He had no choice but to accept his captors' terms and see where it led.

"A wise decision," the voice said, "Would you like some nourishment?"

Dazzled by his alien surroundings and these telepathic beings, Hazbog hadn't realized how hungry he was. The months of hibernation left him famished.

"Yes, I would like something to eat."

"These are from your vessel," the voice reassured as several tubes of food paste appeared at Hazbog's feet, "we took all that you had on board your ship. Our atomic compilers have analyzed the contents, and we now have the ability to produce your sustenance tubes on demand."

"Do you plan to keep me as a pet or zoological exhibit?" Hazbog demanded as he voraciously consumed every tube in sight.

"We do not wish to do either. You will be our guest for as long as you choose to obey The Ten Laws, and we believe you will find it quite easy to do so in our society. Rest now. We will arrive on Aaptuu 4 shortly."

With these final words, the portal door closed and Hazbog was once again alone. He noticed the room he was in suddenly grow a bit smaller. Soon it collapsed around him and he was sealed in a metal cocoon.

Le-Wa and Chi-Col busied themselves with preparations for their journey. They too would be mold casted for their short trip to Aaptuu 4. Mold casting was developed by the Aaptuuans to combat dark matter drive sickness. The Aaptuuans found that during various stages of dark matter transit, organic life forms could become partially disassembled and haphazardly reassembled – sometimes with disastrous results.

Experiments with early versions of mold casting found that molecular scrambling could be prevented by surrounding living tissue with resistomorphic metals.

Aaptuuan scientists made additional modifications to the metal alloys to allow the passage of life supporting gases and to provide maximum comfort during the chaotic trip. Mold casting took some getting used to, but it was far better than being molecularly scrambled.

With a wave of Le-Wa's hand, each was enveloped in a metallic cocoon. Their ship stretched like a long silver band and disappeared into the endless darkness of space. A wonderful tingling sensation tickled every millimeter of Hazbog's body, but no sooner had Hazbog begun to contemplate how strangely he felt did he slip into unconsciousness.

"Welcome to Aaptuu," a voice announced over the intercom.

Le-Wa and Chi-Col's metallic cocoons slowly opened into two silver chairs.

"Has our guest been prepared for transfer?" the voice inquired.

Chi-Col answered groggily, "The mold casting has placed our guest in a recuperative state. We are applying minimal sedation to ensure a smooth transfer."

"We've taken control of your craft and will guide you in from here. Craft logistics out."

Aaptuu 4 was always a beautiful sight. Its vast blue oceans popped dramatically against the red and green forests that lined the continents and surrounded the sparkling silver cities.

"Greetings, Le-Wa and Chi-Col. You must be weary from your journey. We have analyzed your transmissions and made accommodations for our guest. The Council requests your presence in 1725 cycles. It is then you will receive your next mission. Eat and rest my friends. Welcome home."

"Thank you, Dr. VaaCaam-a," Le-Wa said reverently, "We will see you soon."

Their ship was guided into a hanger and set gently down on a large circular landing platform. Several Aaptuuans accompanied by a contingent of short blue aliens entered the craft. They greeted Le-Wa and Chi-Col warmly as the short blue aliens went about the business of transferring Hazbog to his new quarters. As soon they were all gone, Le-Wa and Chi-Col said their goodbyes.

They returned to their homes and ate and rested. When the appointed cycle was upon them, a gently swirling vortex appeared in the center of their respective dwellings. Each stepped in his and was whisked to The Garden.

"Welcome, Le-Wa and Chi-Col. Thank you for your service to the Eelshak System. It is always tragic when a species extinguishes itself, but to do so in such a fashion..."

Dr. VaaCaam-a paused for a moment and bowed his head as he reflected upon the utter devastation caused by the black hole generator.

"Their voices will never be heard again," he said. There was a sober hum of agreement from the council members. All bowed their heads and took a moment of silence.

"Let us say no more of the Eelshakians," Dr. VaaCaam-a began, "We must turn our discussion to Solaris 3. Solaris is located near the outer rim of the fifth arm of Caslu. Solaris 3 is a rocky planet with a nitrogen oxygen atmosphere, a large ocean covering most of its surface. It is emerging from its last Ice Age.

"Suprema is developing metallurgy, agriculture, husbandry, and hiving. We estimate that Suprema will develop interstellar capability in 3,724 years relative to their sun. You will take The Ten Laws to them. While they are often barbaric and cruel, Solaria Suprema can also be kind and loving. Their evolution as a cooperative herd in the face of an unforgivably deadly world has engendered this paradox. We will provide them guidance and they will choose a path. May they choose the righteous path. May The White Light guide you both."

Chapter 4
One Giant Leap

"Do you think it'll work?" Ravi asked Jett as he looked incredulously at the odd device. "I already told you it works," Jett answered impatiently, "Wait and see." "It's a bunch of b.s." Jack said smugly, "Jett, it's funny how you're the only one who's seen this invention of yours in action."

"I showed both of you the video I took of it working."

"Right, as if you couldn't doctor a video," Jack scoffed.

"Well, you're about to see it work right now you jackass," Jett retorted, "I just need to make a couple of adjustments. It's a very delicate machine, you know."

Jett turned a screw here and tweaked a knob there. He checked hoses and valves. He tinkered with the machine like a mad scientist. He double and triple checked every setting, owing Jett knew that a slight misstep could spell disaster.

The other two boys waited in anticipation. Ravi sat at the end of Jett's bed watching his every move and trying to understand how the machine worked. Jack stood in the corner of the bedroom, half watching Jett and half staring out the window at a pick-up game of street hockey the neighborhood kids were playing below in the cul-de-sac.

"Why can't you be more like other kids?" Jack teased. "All you want to do is sit in your room all day and build weird stuff. Why don't we go outside and play some hockey? It looks like they could use a few more players."

"You can go if you like," Jett replied coolly.

16

"I will," Jack snorted, "right after I watch that stupid machine of yours blow up in your face, Mr. Ty-D-Bol!" Jack laughed riotously for a few moments crossing his arms and raising his left eyebrow as high as he could to further drive home his point. "Well, let's see it already," he insisted.

"One sec..." a distracted Jett shot back.

Jett's room was noticeably different from those of most eighth graders. The first thing one noticed upon entering it was the odd shape of the room itself. It was octagonal, in that it had eight sides, but the walls were of differing lengths so the whole room seemed wildly disproportioned.

The walls were lined floor to ceiling with wooden shelves that displayed hundreds of bizarre contraptions. If not for the schematics pasted on the ceiling and everywhere else Jett could find free space, it would be impossible to guess what most of these things were intended for. They were universally unusual.

There was the Grappler 3000, a spring loaded grappling hook built into the cut off handle of Jack's favorite aluminum baseball bat. There was a device that looked like a Singer sewing machine that Jett modified to be a laser cutter. There was a ball of wire that looked like a ball of yarn. This was Jett's 'retracto-wire' which did precisely what the name implied.

There were many items that defied description. Some were metallic things merged with wooden things merged with glass things and various crystals and electronics. Others were shaped like pyramids, spheres, or cubes. Still stranger objects combined all three shapes with various tubes, crystals, batteries, and buttons. If not for the radically futuristic appearance of so many of these contraptions, one might believe he was in the presence of Thomas Edison, himself.

"Welllllll... We're waitinggggg," Jack instigated.

"Give him a break," Ravi said, "He's almost ready, right Jett?"

"I'll give you both a break. I'm going outside to play some hockey," Jack sighed.

"Wait," Jett interrupted, "It's ready. Hand me that blue Lego brick."

Ravi leaned back and grabbed the small blue brick from the top of a gray metal file cabinet that Jett used as a bed stand. He had been Jett's best friend since kindergarten, and in all that time, he had never seen Jett so animated. Ravi examined the brick to assess its authenticity.

"Appears to be the real McCoy," he joked as he handed it to Jett.

"Straight from Denmark," Jett smiled.

"Straight from Denmark," Jack mocked rolling his eyes, "Get on with it already!"

"Ok," Jett started, "Here's what we're gonna do. We're going to place the Lego on top of the machine as such." Jett gently placed the blue brick on what could best be described as a playing card sized platform. The platform itself was delicately perched on eight narrow wires that spanned what appeared to be a large silver mixing bowl. Other than the silver bowl, the device was painted school bus yellow and was covered with multicolored buttons and switches. An iTouch mounted on its side acted as the central control mechanism.

"Now you two stand over there by the dresser. I'm gonna beam this blue brick into the chimney of that Lego house over there." Jett pointed to the far corner of his room.

Jack and Ravi's eyes followed Jett's finger to an old three legged stool holding a little Lego cottage complete with garden, trees, and a white picket fence. A brick was missing from the center of its white chimney. "I'm going to transfer the atoms that make up this Lego brick from the Swap Pad here into the house's chimney. I'll do this via a concept my mom calls 'Quantum Exchange'," Jett explained making quotation marks in the air. "Gentlemen, behold the Quantum Swapper."

"How original, Ty-D-Bol. I think I saw this trick when Mom and Dad took us to see Chris Angel last year in Las Vegas," Jack interrupted as he ran over to the little house and stuck his finger into the hole in the chimney where the Lego was missing. "Let's get this over with already."

"Ha Ha. Now go back over there where it's safe," Jett demanded, "Ok, Ravi can you record this on my tablet?"

"Sure thing," Ravi replied as he looked into the camera screen, changed its direction slightly, and pressed the red button. "Live from San Jose, it's Star Trek, the next, Next Generation."

"Ok, in 5, 4, 3, 2, 1," Jett pressed a button on the side of the machine. Nothing happened at first. Then the machine made a low hum and with an instantaneous flash of light the Lego brick disappeared. When the three looked over at the Lego house, the blue brick was placed perfectly in the white chimney. "What do you think of that?"

"Ummmm..." Ravi stuttered, "How'd you do that?"

"Well," Jett explained, "As I said before, the device moves matter by swapping quantumly entangled particles. My Mom's papers talk all about it. It turns out that entangled particles have some pretty interesting characteristics which make the concept of distance irrelevant."

"How does it work?" Ravi asked curiously.

"These knobs here determine direction," Jett said demoing the machine like a vacuum cleaner salesman, "and I enter the distance in meters into the iTouch. The real trick in making it work is..."

"Oh, come on," Jack interjected, "It's a trick. How'd you *really* do it?"

"It's just like I said, the device swaps matter by..."

"I see," Jack interrupted rushing over to the machine and grabbing the first knob he could, "and these knobs control direction and you enter the distance in here, right?"

"Jack, don't touch it! You'll break it!" Jett protested loudly, "Get away from it!"

Jett lunged at his brother. Jack twisted a knob and quickly punched four digits into the touchscreen. "There, that ought to do it. Take me to Disney World!" Jack shouted.

"Get away from it! You don't know how to use it!" Jett screamed slamming into Jack. Jack fell to the floor. Jett turned away to tend to his machine and Jack kicked him, sending Jett hurtling onto the table. Jett's hand knocked the activation control as he wrapped his arms around his invention in an effort to keep it from crashing on the floor.

At first, nothing happened. Then there was a low hum.

"Jett, put that thing down!" Ravi screamed.

In a flash, Jett and his machine were gone. Every plug exploded with sparks and the entire city's lights dimmed momentarily.

"What the hell just happened?" Jack shouted in a panic, "it's gotta be a trick. He's in here somewhere. Jett, c'mon buddy. Come on out."

Jack and Ravi waited silently for a few seconds.

"Jett, stop messing around..."

Silence.

"Jett?"

Ravi stared at the swirling smoke in shock, tears welling in his eyes.

Jack raced frantically around the large octagonal room. He opened every closet door, but there was no sign of Jett. He looked under the bed. Jett wasn't there.

Jack choked, "there's gotta be a logical explanation."

Unbeknownst to him, Jack's tinkering set the Quantum Swapper's destination coordinates 7,888 kilometers away and 5 kilometers high, and that's precisely where Jett reappeared moments later.

One second Jett was in his bedroom showing off his new Quantum Swapper, and the very next he was plummeting toward the earth at terminal velocity!

"Ahhhhhhhhhhhhhhhhhhhhhhhhhhhhh!" Jett screamed, clutching his invention and tumbling head over heels toward the ocean below.

Chapter 5
A Close Encounter

Jett had always wanted to skydive. He and Ravi discussed it many times over the years, but Jett never imagined it would go down like this. He desperately wished his invention could somehow beam him a perfectly packed parachute, or at the very least swap him back to his room, but without a power source, it was useless.

Feeling the need to make peace as his life flashed before his eyes, Jett forgave his brother for being such a jerk and inadvertently killing him. He also acknowledged that he never should have read his mom's physics papers in the first place.

"Jack's just jealous dad gave me his dog tags," Jett thought.

Even with his death inevitable, Jett didn't feel frightened. He didn't feel alone. He felt a presence there with him.

A warm voice whispered in his mind. Jett thought the voice to be that of an Angel welcoming him to the afterlife.

"Jett," the soothing voice said, "You will be with us soon. Everything will be ok."

He was enveloped by a warm white light. His muscles relaxed. The light grew brighter until it blinded him even with his eyes shut.

"You are with us now. You are safe," the voice welcomed.

Jett felt his body slow to a stop and begin floating upward!

He thought, "Is this what it's like to be dead?"

If so, it wasn't so bad, Jett contemplated, in fact, it was quite pleasant. The light was warm, like sunshine on a clear spring day. Jett felt euphoric. He felt free as he floated up into the sky.

"You are not dead, Jett," the voice answered, "You joined us onboard our craft."

"What? Craft? What craft?"

"All of your questions will be answered, Jett. Relax. You are safe with us."

Was he dreaming? It seemed so surreal. Not thirty seconds ago Jett was in his room showing off his latest invention and now he was being held aboard some unknown craft. Who was behind this voice in his head if not God or some angel to welcome him to heaven or hell or to wherever one plummeting toward earth at terminal velocity without a parachute might find himself after he hit the ground?

Jett felt the air pass him. The bright light eased and he found himself in some sort of an airlock. The space seemed at once finite and infinite. Other than the door he entered, the airlock itself lacked any depth or definition. The door disappeared and Jett floated weightless in the space.

Though the walls around him seemed very near, when Jett reached out, he could not touch them. It was as if they retreated from his fingers.

"Am I Tantalus? Will you make me stand in water beneath a fruit tree with low hanging branches?" Jett demanded.

"No, Jett. We will not deprive you of nourishment as your mythological Zeus did his own son - unfortunately, a

23

scenario not so uncommon on your planet even today," the voice replied.

"My planet? You are not from Earth?"

"We are not of your world, but we've been watching your species for some time and know more about you than you can possibly imagine. Please relax your body, Jett. It will make the transfer much easier on you."

"How can I relax? I've been kidnapped!"

"It's not a requirement, Jett, but relaxation is highly recommended for your comfort and wellbeing."

Jett tried to relax, but the warm comfortable sensation he was feeling moments before was replaced by cold uncertainty and fear. He didn't understand what was happening to him, but Jett understood one thing: he best listen to his captors and begin relaxing immediately if he was interested in his 'comfort and wellbeing.'

Jett closed his eyes. He took slow deep breaths like those he had seen in his mom's yoga videos. He let his arms and legs go loose. He slowly wiggled his fingers and toes until they dangled limply.

"Excellent," the voice reassured, "The transfer will be easy for you."

Then the walls closed in on him. Jett found himself in a metallic cocoon. He felt the awkward sensation of moving through the metal. In less than a minute by his reckoning, he was in a large empty chamber. Like the airlock, this room lacked definition. If not for the floor he was standing on, he would have been unable to distinguish up from down; left from right; back from forth.

"Welcome, Jett," the voice began, "You are a very lucky

boy. We detected some unexpected quantum disturbances on your planet and were compelled to investigate. Had this been your first quantum exchange, you would have most certainly plummeted to your death."

"You detected my quantum disturbances?" Jett asked inquisitively.

"Indeed, and they were quite unexpected at this point in your species socio-technological time line. Their very existence poses a major problem for your species and the galaxy at large."

"What kind of problem?" Jett pressed.

No sooner had Jett asked his question, a door opened in the wall. Two beings entered the chamber. Other than the color of the gems on their silver necklaces, Jett could not distinguish one from the other.

They both were pale white in color with large heads and small bodies. They had two arms and two legs like a human, but their faces were shaped liked guitar picks and were supported on their short bodies by thin featureless necks. They each had two large teardrop shaped black eyes complemented by two minuscule nostrils and a small mouth.

Jett stared in disbelief. Had he watched too many late night alien abduction documentaries on the History Channel? He swore that when he woke up, he'd never watch another one of those stupid shows ever again for as long as he lived.

"You are not dreaming, Jett," the voice said, "We are very real and you are very much here with us flying 321.82 kilometers above your planet's surface."

"Which one of you said that?"

"I did," Le-Wa answered telepathically while raising his

left arm.

"You can speak to me in my thoughts. How do you do that?"

"Our species can do many things yours cannot," Le-Wa replied, "Yet you possess something that your species can do that we cannot."

"My invention?"

"Yes. We would like you to give it to us so that we may examine it."

Jett's arms unconsciously tightened around his device.

"There's no need to fear us," Le-Wa continued, "We want to help you. We need to insure that your device does not propagate."

"You're going to steal my quantum swapper!" Jett exclaimed gripping his device ever tighter.

"No," Chi-Col interrupted while raising his right hand, "we are attempting to save your world."

"What do you mean?"

"We mean to spare your planet the fate of others who stumble upon interstellar technology before they are ready."

"Interstellar?" Jett thought, "I was just swapping legos in my room, how could my invention be used for interstellar anything?"

"Yes, Jett," Chi-Col agreed, "It is true. You understand not what you toy with. Your species' haphazard trial and error approach to science when applied to a device with such capabilities as this will prove disastrous. If you will not surrender the device, you leave us no choice but to take it from you."

Chapter 6
The Ten Laws

Jett opened his eyes, sat up, and looked around. He was back in his room.

"Whew," Jett sighed, "It was just a dream, a weird crazy dream... a nightmare."

Jett jumped out of bed. He rushed over to the Swapper. The blue Lego sat in the center of the Swap Pad. He looked over at the Lego house in the corner of his room.

"With a little tinkering, I can land the brick perfectly in the chimney."

Legos were the obvious choice for Jett's experiments due to their interlocking nature. Plus using them lessened the burden on his 3D printer.

He knew that if he could place a single Lego into the center of a stack of interlocked bricks, like the chimney on the little house, then he could control the swapping process with absolute precision. What his stupid brother didn't realize when he started fiddling around with the switches and buttons was that precision was everything in swapping. One wrong move and you could end up swapped in the center of a mountain, at the bottom of the ocean, or theoretically find yourself gasping for air on the moon.

It was then that he remembered he never went to bed. He remembered fighting with Jack. He remembered falling from the sky. Was it possible that he was knocked out when he hit the machine and was subsequently carried off to bed by Jack and Ravi? If so, falling from the sky was nothing more than a dream. But then again, how did the blue brick make it back to the sensor? Hadn't he swapped it into the chimney just before he blacked out? Something wasn't adding up.

Inexplicably, his surroundings morphed. His octagonal bedroom and its collection of strange devices, sculptures, and belongings melted into the walls. Within moments, he stood in the center of a silver metallic room. The room lacked definition of any kind. It had no edges or corners and seemed at once confined and infinite.

"One called, Jett," a voice said, "Welcome."

Jett recognized the voice. It was the one that had spoken to him while he was falling. A door opened. In shuffled two chalk white aliens with large black eyes. It came rushing back to him.

Jett muttered, "Is this for real?"

"Yes, Jett. Your experience is real. You are not dreaming."

"...And you pulled me out of the sky?"

"We arrived in time. You were lucky."

"Why are you holding me prisoner? I haven't done anything to you."

"Jett, you are not our prisoner. You are our guest."

"Why do you keep me here?"

"Your quantum swapper, Jett," Le-Wa replied raising his left hand. "It is both beautiful and dangerous."

"Dangerous? How?"

"It puts your species at risk of neutralization," Le-Wa continued, "You see, Jett, we have observed your planet for many thousands of years. Yours is the last of two potential space faring species on your planet. Unfortunately, your invention comes too soon in the evolutionary time line of your species. Your discovery of fission makes you dangerous enough, but now the quantum swapper gives your species the potential to transport fission weapons anywhere in the universe instantaneously. Your warlike tendencies and proclivity toward inequality and thuggery have The Fold very concerned."

"Two space faring species on my planet? What's the other one, dolphins?"

"The other animal on your planet with space faring potential is Solaris Gigantis, the one you call Yeti or Sasquatch. Today they are very few in number and are likely to follow the rest of your family tree into extinction. Solaris Gigantis has only survived this long because it's evolved to avoid your species."

"You're telling me Bigfoot is real? I didn't know aliens could be conspiracy theorists."

"Not only is your so-called Bigfoot real, it is the only creature on Solaris 3 currently abiding by all of The Ten Laws."

"What are The Ten Laws?"

"They are," Le-Wa explained,

"Do not kill others.

Do not steal from others.

Do not lie to others.

Do not sow discord among others.

Do not feel envy for others' possessions.

Do not act selfishly.

Do not hold hatred in your heart.

Honor your forebears.

Honor your offspring.

Love everything.

"Your species, Jett, has a very hard time following

these laws even though it would benefit greatly by doing so."

"Don't kill. Don't steal. Don't lie," Jett thought, everyone knows those, "but there were a couple in there I didn't quite recognize."

"You know them well enough," Chi-Col telepathed.

"I really wish you would stop talking in my head!" Jett complained, "It's freaking me out."

"We can't help it Jett, it's our natural method of communication."

"Can you read each other's minds?"

"Of course. We have nothing to hide from one another. Your species is a dozen short generations from achieving telepathic communication. It would be a shame if you weren't around to enjoy it."

"Why wouldn't we be around?" Jett inquired nervously.

"There is too much hate; too much distrust; too little love," Le-Wa telepathed sadly.

"Your species' chances of surviving the next 150 years are estimated at less than 5%," Chi-Col added.

"Yes," Le-Wa agreed, "but many of our galactic compatriots faced higher odds."

"True," thought Chi-Col, "of course, his device changes everything."

"Indeed it does. Jett," Le-Wa continued, "Do you know how long Chi-Col and I have been assigned to your planet?"

"I don't know... Ummm, fifty years? Maybe sixty?"

Le-Wa and Chi-Col shared a glance and seemed to smirk at each other.

"No, Jett, Chi-Col and I were assigned to your planet,

Solaris 3 as we know it, some 3,500 of your years ago, but The Fold has observed and recorded, at intervals, almost 30,000 years of your planet's evolution. Our assignment here has been an interesting one. Your planet is unique in many ways."

"So how old are each of you?"

"In your years, I'm 14,526," Chi-Col answered.

"And I'm 18,834 as you would understand it," Le-Wa added.

Jett stood in awe. How could these beings standing before him be older than Shakespeare, older then Julius Caesar, older then Plato, Moses, the Pyramids? Heck, older than human civilization itself? "How is this possible?" he asked.

"The Ten Laws make everything possible as you will soon learn," Le-Wa replied. "We are taking you with us to Aaptuu 4 to see the High Council. They would like to meet the being responsible for creating quantum exchange."

"Will I ever see Earth again? My family?" Jett begged.

"Yes you will," Chi-Col answered, "but it will never again be as you remember it."

"What do you mean?"

"You will see for yourself when the time comes."

"What's that supposed to mean?"

"I cannot explain it to you. You must experience it for yourself in order to truly understand. Regardless of what happens to Solaris 3 now, it will never again be the same for you, Jett. Now, we must ready ourselves for the journey to Aaptuu 4. Please sit in that chair and close your eyes." Le-Wa said as he motioned to Jett's left. "Doing so will make the journey much more comfortable for you."

Jett turned his head and a silver metallic chair formed

itself out of the floor. Without protest, Jett sat down in the chair and shut his eyes tightly.

"Good," Le-Wa encouraged, "You will do well in Oonuua, Capitol of Aaptuu 4."

Jett thought about the chamber he was in and the two aliens and his impending interstellar journey. He agreed. Whatever the outcome, his life would never be the same again.

Chapter 7
Something About Bob

Jett, Le-Wa, and Chi-Col arrived on Aaptuu 4 with little fanfare. The trip itself seemed incredibly short to Jett. Other than his being enveloped inside a metallic cocoon, which he surmised would take some getting used to, the journey was surprisingly comfortable. By Jett's reckoning, the entire trip couldn't have taken more than 15 minutes, but there was no way to be sure.

Jett spent most of the trip intensely focused on the strange tingling that tickled every millimeter of his body. It felt as though he was being pulled apart and put back together over and over again. The experience left Jett exhausted beyond anything he had ever known and as the metallic cocoon opened, he passed out and collapsed to the floor.

On the ship's bridge, Le-Wa and Chi-Col emerged from their cocoons and gave the controls over to Flight Logistics in Oonuua. Dr. VaaCaam-a appeared on the wall before them.

"Le-Wa... Chi-Col... Welcome home. I know you were not expecting to return so soon, but The Council understands that recent events on Solaris 3 have altered the course of your assignment."

"Yes, they have, VaaCaam-a" Le-Wa replied, "We have the Solarian Jett and his quantum exchanger in our care."

"You are to escort him to Tower 100. We have prepared his quarters. Bring the quantum exchanger directly to the council for examination. We look forward to seeing you both shortly."

"Thank you, VaaCaam-a," Le-Wa said.

Dr. VaaCaam-a nodded his head and his image dissolved into that of Aaptuu 4's tranquil blue oceans and green, red, and silver continents.

"It's beautiful," Chi-Col stated, "How I missed it."

"As did I," Le-Wa agreed.

"What do you surmise will be the fate of Solaris 3?"

"It's a difficult problem, Chi-Col. There is so much good, so much potential being held back by so few with too loud a voice. Those same few who would take the quantum exchanger and pervert it to their own selfish ends hold the key to its fate."

"And what of the peaceful Solaris Gigantis?"

"The council may do as it has done in other systems where similar disparity exists. Of course, Gigantis would suffer little in the aftermath of neutralization."

While Le-Wa and Chi-Col pondered the fate of Solaris 3, their ship was guided smoothly through the troposphere of Aaptuu 4, through its pink and orange clouds, and into one of the flight paths above Oonuua. Tower 100 loomed in the distance.

They flew between the tall silver towers of Oonuua with their bountiful balcony gardens. Every shade of green, red, blue, brown, purple, pink, magenta, yellow, and orange cast itself in the warm light of the rising sun.

"Look at all of that delicious food," Chi-Col telepathed, "There is nothing like a home-grown meal."

Le-Wa returned the sentiment with a wide grin.

They soon arrived at Tower 100. With Jett now asleep, the ship set itself down on a large circular landing platform. A door opened on the craft's underside and a ramp extended to the platform's deck. There several Aaptuuans and blue Suprema Domestica waited patiently. They entered the ship with quick precision.

The Suprema Domestica or Domes (pronounced 'dough-maze', for short) quickly collected a sleeping Jett and placed him on a floating gurney. They quietly ferried him off to his quarters in Tower 100.

While he slept onboard the ship, Le-Wa and Chi-Col conducted extensive mental and physical examinations. This information was then transmitted, interpreted, and integrated into Jett's dwelling.

His dwelling then utilized the data to create a mirror image of Jett's intellectual potential and inclination toward positive or negative choices. His thoughts and desires determined how his dwelling would manifest itself physically and provide for his wants and needs.

Whether an inhabitant of Tower 100 awoke in heaven or hell was entirely up to the unconscious mind of that Dweller, as Tower 100's residents were known. In most cases, with sufficient counseling and time, Dwellers crafted pleasant and productive existences – often extending their lifespans many centuries in the process.

When Jett opened his eyes, he was being carried down a brightly lit featureless hallway. He turned his head to the right and saw a strange blue being walking beside him. Another walked to his left and there were two more by his feet.

Jett tried to say something, but his mouth wouldn't open, and although he didn't appear to be bound to the gurney, he could not move his arms or his legs. He couldn't even wiggle his fingers or toes. The only thing he could do was watch in silence as the seemingly endless hallway passed by.

Jett remembered the ship and the silver chamber and the two aliens that had spoken to him in his thoughts, but these were not the chalky white aliens he remembered. Their skin was pale blue. These beings also appeared shorter than the white ones and had smaller heads in proportion to their bodies. Jett wondered if, like the others, these beings could read his mind. He waited for a response, but none came. Jett projected his thoughts more deliberately.

"I wonder if they can read my thoughts..."

Jett waited a moment. Silence. Nothing. The blue aliens simply stared straight ahead as they walked. After what seemed to Jett like a very long time, the procession stopped. Jett looked to his left and saw a yellowish white light take the shape of a door. It opened slowly and the four beings ushered him inside.

As Jett crossed the threshold, he realized he was back in his own room! He felt jubilant for a moment before remembering the same scenario played out previously on the space craft.

"I'm not falling for this again!" Jett thought defiantly. "How stupid do you think I am?"

"No one here believes you to be of low intelligence, Dweller Jett. Especially for a Solarian," a voice in his head replied.

"Which one of you is speaking to me?" Jett demanded of the four blue aliens.

"It is none of them, Dweller Jett. They cannot communicate with you yet."

"Why not?"

"They cannot understand your thoughts. Your thought waves are indecipherable to Domes. They have never seen a Solarian before and your thoughts sound to them as Russian or Greek might sound to you. In time, their brains will adjust to your wave patterns and they will be better able to assist you."

"Assist me? I thought I was a prisoner," Jett stated flatly as the Domes lifted him from the gurney, placed him on his bed, and quickly exited the room without a sound. "Where are they going?"

"So many questions, Dweller Jett. You will be an interesting guest to please."

"Stop calling me your guest. Is that your way of saying 'prisoner'?"

"So much distrust. This is a problem with your species. It, too, will fade with time. Now, Dweller Jett, you must be hungry. What would you like to eat?"

"Why do you keep calling me Dweller Jett?"

"I call you Dweller Jett because that is who you are."

"No, my name is Jett Javelin, Jett Joseph Javelin Jr."

"Yes, you are, but here you will be known as Dweller Jett."

"You don't understand. Jett is my first name. Joseph is my middle name. Javelin is my last name, and I'm a 'junior' because my dad named me after himself, and I have his dog tags to prove it."

"Ok, I have reprogrammed myself to address you as Dweller Jett Joseph Javelin Junior."

"That's not what I'm saying. What I meant was..."

"Would you like something to eat Dweller Jett Joseph Javelin Junior?"

"Can you please just call me Jett?"

"Whatever you wish Dweller Jett Joseph Javelin Junior."

"You did it again. Ugh. Ok. I'll have something to eat. What are my choices?"

"Your choices are virtually infinite. May I suggest some of your favorites?"

"Um, sure..."

"Your grandmother's lasagna is always an excellent choice. You also quite enjoy VeggieGrill. Or perhaps you'd like..."

"Can you really make my grandmother's lasagna?"

"I can make it as you remember it, Dweller Jett."

"Ok. I'll have some lasagna please," Jett said clasping his hands together in front of himself.

"That's an interesting gesture. I suppose you are begging for lasagna. There's no need to beg here. All of your needs will be provided for. Would you like your entree in the parlor or on the terrace, Dweller Jett?"

"Terrace? My room doesn't have a terrace."

"Your 'room', Dweller Jett, is a reflection of your unconscious mind."

Jett turned his head to where the little Lego house should be. It was not there. In its place was a large open door where a wall was supposed to be. Jett sat up in bed.

"I can move."

"Your mobility has been restored," the voice stated. "Would you like your entree on the terrace or in the..."

"...Parlor. On the terrace please," Jett meekly interrupted as he stood up and walked to the terrace in awe.

Otherwise, not one single feature in his bedroom had changed. Everything was exactly as he remembered except for the terrace. He cautiously stuck his head outside.

"No freakin' way," he whispered stepping outside and into an alien civilization. He was surrounded by hundreds if not thousands of tall silver blue towers. Every tower had plants growing down from it. They were of every imaginable color, and the colors popped brightly in the glistening sun. Silver space craft flew harmoniously through the blue green sky as if to some unheard musical rhythm.

"What is this place?" Jett asked wondrously.

"Oonuua. It is the heart of the Aaptuuan civilization. The Seat of The Fold."

"Seat of The Fold? What is this Fold you all keep talking about?"

"Eat, Dweller Jett, and rest. You'll need your strength for The Council. They will answer your questions."

Jett looked down from the city skyline and there on a table before him was a heaping portion of his grandmother's lasagna. It was plated just right, with napkin, fork, and an ice cold Dr. Pepper complete with condensation running down the can.

"Nice presentation," Jett marveled.

"Eat, Dweller Jett. Eat while there is time."

Jett had been so enthralled by his new surroundings, he hadn't realized how hungry he was. He rushed to the table, sat down, and ravenously attacked the lasagna. It was delicious! Even better than he remembered. Jett gobbled down every bite and immediately turned his attention to the Dr. Pepper. Parched, he chugged the soda down, wiped his mouth, and slammed the empty can down on the bistro table.

"Buuuuuuuuurrrp!" Jett belched loudly, "that was amazing! Can I have more?"

"As you wish, Dweller Jett."

Much to Jett's surprise another plate of lasagna and a fresh Dr. Pepper appeared on the table.

"No way!" Jett blurted out.

"Yes, way," the voice replied. "You require more nourishment than I calculated. I have made note of it, Dweller Jett."

"Excellent, ummm, what's your name?" Jett asked as he dug into the delectable dish.

"What would you like it to be?"

"Let's see. Alfred's taken. Jeeves is too obvious. How about Bob?"

"Bob it is, Dweller Jett."

The doorbell rang.

"My bedroom has a doorbell?"

"Should I answer it, Dweller Jett?"

"Of course, um, errr, Bob. You should answer it."

"As you wish."

Jett placed his fork down on the table and turned toward the door. Two pale white aliens walked out onto the terrace.

"Jett, how are you adapting to your dwelling?"

"Le-Wa is that you?"

"Yes it is, and Chi-Col is with me."

Jett carefully examined the crystal pendants that dangled on delicate silver chains from each of their necks. "Yeah, I guessed it was you two, but honestly I can't tell any of you apart."

"Perhaps this will help," Le-Wa offered.

Le-Wa morphed into a tall black man in a black suit with a white shirt and a blue tie. He had short white hair and a neatly trimmed beard to match. Chi-Col transformed into a Japanese man of medium height with straight black hair and wore a navy blue suit with a red bow tie and shiny black shoes.

"Yup, that does it," Jett said mystified. "How did you do that?"

"We simply altered your dwelling's frequency to change your perception of us. Are you satisfied with its performance?" Le-Wa asked.

"Performance? You mean my room?"

"Yes, your room. Has it been to your satisfaction?"

"Truthfully, I'd prefer my old room, but this one's OK as far as artificially intelligent bedrooms on strange alien planets go."

"But I've done everything you've asked of me," Bob interrupted, "and we've known each other for so little a time."

Jett rolled his eyes. "It's nothing you've done, Bob. I'd just prefer to be home with my family." Jett turned his attention back to the Aaptuuans. "Judging from your attire, I'm taking it you're not here for a social visit."

The Aaptuuans looked at each other, then at each other's suits and replied, "Our thoughts betray us. We are here to take you to see the High Council of Oonuua. You may finish your nourishment before we leave if you require."

"I've kinda lost my appetite," Jett said flatly.

"Then let us go to The Garden," Le-Wa finished.

Le-Wa and Chi-Col morphed back to their natural

selves. They guided Jett through his bedroom and outside into the mysterious and featureless hallway. Jett could not discern up from down and he stumbled to the floor.

Le-Wa helped Jett get back to his feet and instructed him to close his eyes. Jett did as he was told. "You will hold each of our hands. We will guide you. In time, your mind will adapt to Tower 100 and it in turn will adapt to yours."

They walked for a long time, but Jett dared not open his eyes. Ultimately, he knew that he would end up at the same destination whether or not he could see where they were going. He thought about the Aaptuuans' hands. They were a lot warmer than he expected. Jett listened intently, but he couldn't hear a sound other than that of wind rushing past his ears.

Finally, Jett heard a click and felt a strong swoosh of air. He heard something like birds singing. His eyelids lit up so much that he shut them even tighter to counter the sudden brightness.

"Can I open my eyes now?" he asked his companions.

"You may," Le-Wa responded.

Jett opened his eyes. They were surrounded by a lush garden. Tower 100 itself was so tall that it disappeared into the clouds above. Jett stared in amazement at the strange collection of plants, animals, and insects.

"This way, Jett," Chi-Col urged.

They walked a short distance through the garden and soon came to a grand amphitheater.

"We are here," Le-Wa stated, "The Council will arrive momentarily."

Chapter 8
The Great Escape

Jett watched blue and yellow insects flutter about and pollinate all manner of strange alien flowers. The plants brimmed with odd looking fruit of every imaginable hue. Vines climbed the walls and lined the walkways of the enormous amphitheater.

Le-Wa walked up to a small tree. He picked off a football shaped fruit wrapped with alternating chocolate brown and beige stripes. He poked two holes in it, tilted his head back, and carefully emptied its contents into his mouth. He then placed the empty husk at the base of the tree and took a step back. The earth beneath the husk slowly shifted and shook. The husk sank silently into the ground leaving no trace.

"What happened to the husk?" Jett asked.

"It was reabsorbed by the plant," Le-wa answered.

"Will it do that to me?!"

"No, Jett. You have nothing to fear. The plants willingly and generously provide nourishment. They will not harm you."

"Willingly? Plants? You mean, they're conscious?"

"Not as you understand it, Jett, but yes, they are 'aware' if that is what you mean," Chi-Col offered.

Their conversation was suddenly cut short by a soft whirring sound emanating from somewhere below the amphitheater. The outline of a large double doorway appeared in the wall directly behind the first row of 'seats'.

"They are here," Le-Wa announced.

"Who is here?"

The doors opened wide and Aaptuuans and Domes

filed in by the thousand. The Aaptuuans walked directly to their seats while the Domes acted as Ushers and took up positions at the end of every row. Jett marveled at the efficiency with which thousands of beings coordinated their efforts. In the time it would take humans to board a commercial airline flight these beings filled an amphitheater larger than any he knew to exist on Earth.

The shuffling of the feet ceased all at once. An ominous silence followed. Jett felt unnerved, "What are they going to do with me?" Jett whispered.

"We are also curious to see what The Council will do with you," Le-Wa stated matter of factly.

Jett heard a single set of footsteps emanating from the doorway. A solitary Aaptuuan emerged. This Aaptuuan was identical to all the rest with one exception, it sported a thin gold ring around its head. The ring was a simple gold band the width of a pinky finger. It reminded Jett of a halo. The being approached Jett.

"One they call Jett Joseph Javelin Junior, we would like to welcome you to Oonuua. We understand that you have come a very long way to be with us today. My name is Dr. VaaCaam-a."

"What do you want from me?" Jett asked shyly.

"Jett, this is not about me and you or us and them. We have brought you here to determine whether you are capable of saving your species from itself, from neutralization, and from possible extinction."

"What are you talking about?"

"The device you made poses an existential threat to your planet and all of its life forms, because it allows your

44

species to extend its destructive behavior far beyond the reaches of your own solar system. The Fold will not allow this. To do so is a violation of The Ten Laws and our charter to maintain interstellar peace."

"How does my invention do that?"

"In your hands, the quantum exchanger is of little concern to us. In fact, it has great potential to enhance the evolution of your species both biologically and socially. The medical applications alone are infinite, but there is too great a chance your device will fall into the wrong hands. There are still many Solarians driven by avarice, greed, and lust for power. If the denizens of your planet do not exterminate themselves first, they are likely to use your device to exterminate others. The question, Jett, is how are you going to stop them?"

A low hum of agreement echoed through the amphitheater. Dr. VaaCaam-a turned toward the Aaptuuan council and bowed his head reverently.

He then turned back to Jett and said, "Before you answer, we feel you lack the facts necessary to place the gravity of your situation into the proper context." Dr. VaaCaam-a paused for dramatic effect.

After a few moments he continued, "Since long before your most primitive settlements, The Fold has observed your planet, Solaris 3, as it is commonly known. While your planet is blessed with a rich variety of life forms, it is not unique in our Universe. There are billions of planets that boast rich zoological variety and tens of millions with intelligent life forms. Our charge, that of The Fold, is to maintain interstellar peace and harmony.

"We are pleased to inform you that The Fold is

currently comprised of 1,756,234 of the most intelligent and peaceful species discovered to date. All member species abide by the tenets of The Ten Laws. Those that do not follow The Ten Laws are subject to ongoing evaluation. Malcontent species whose intentions are bent on inequality and destruction are allowed to exercise free will, so long as their chaotic behavior remains contained within the bounds of their home system."

Dr. VaaCaam-a paused to read Jett's reaction. Jett stood stoically as the weight of the world was cast upon him.

"It is to these species we bring The Ten Laws as we did to yours some 3,500 of your years ago. It is not unusual for primitive intelligents to take several hundred generations to comply with The Ten Laws. Evolution can be a slow and cumbersome process. Your civilization is just 141.42 generations along and is on the cusp of a great enlightenment. It would be a shame to end the trial so soon."

"What do you mean 'end the trial'?" Jett wondered aloud.

"If another Solaria Suprema obtains your device, your planet will be neutralized."

"You mean you'll kill everybody?"

"No, we will neutralize your electronics. It is true some will die, but your species will likely live on, and with some luck earn a second chance to enter The Fold. Most importantly, your destructive habits will be contained for the time being."

"You have me and the quantum swapper here with you. Shouldn't that be enough? No one else on my planet knows how to build one."

"Not true, Jett," Dr. VaaCaam-a replied. "You left a set

of plans on your bed and a video recording of your disappearance. As we speak, your mother is reviewing these and attempting to reverse engineer what happened to you."

A holographic image of Evelyn Javelin projected into the center of the amphitheater. Surrounded by dozens of staff, she carefully examined Jett's quantum swapper blueprints in her lab. She squinted at them intensely, determined to understand what happened to Jett.

"Mom, I'm ok," Jett called out, but the image of his mother quickly faded and was replaced with that of Dr. VaaCaam-a.

"According to our mind scan, you built your machine using theories derived from your mother's papers. Therefore, she is not only capable of replicating the device, but driven to do so by the fierce love of a mother. We estimate she will have such a replica in 47 Solarian days."

"Then we should bring her here," Jett suggested, "...with the plans."

"I'm afraid that's not possible, Jett. She has shown your designs to others. They too are racing to replicate your discovery. The proverbial genie is out of the bottle."

"Ok, what can I do to fix this?"

"That is for you to decide."

"You're not even going to give me a hint or suggestion as to what I'm supposed to do? You're the super advanced race, right? You gotta help me."

"We will help you once you have chosen a particular course of action," Dr. VaaCaam-a replied patiently. "You will now be escorted to your Dwelling where you will decide."

Dr. VaaCaam-a turned his back to Jett and walked to

47

the doorway. Before he exited the amphitheater, he turned to Jett and said, "The Fold has every confidence you will choose the right path for your people."

"That makes one of us," Jett shot back, but Dr. VaaCaam-a had already disappeared through the door. He was quickly followed by the rest of the council and Domes. Soon the amphitheater was empty except for Jett and his guides.

Jett turned to his companions and pleaded, "What am I supposed to do?"

Le-Wa grabbed Jett by the hand and said, "Your path will reveal itself as you go. The answers will present themselves as you pursue the questions. You must trust your instincts. Now you will return to your Dwelling."

With that Jett was escorted back to Tower 100 and through the seemingly endless hallways that led back to Bob. Back in his dwelling, Le-Wa turned to Jett and said, "May your journey be a successful one. Your system is depending on you." Then he and Chi-Col exited and closed the door behind them.

"No pressure then," he muttered to himself, "when did saving the Earth become my problem? I'm just a kid!"

"Dweller Jett, I'm pleased you have returned. How may I be of assistance?" Bob asked.

"You can turn back time and make it so I never built that stupid quantum swapper in the first place," Jett pleaded.

"I cannot do that for you, Dweller Jett. That would be theoretically impossible. Would you like some more lasagna?"

"No I don't want any more lasagna. How can I eat at a time like this?"

"Perhaps you would like something else?"

Jett thought about it for a moment and then he said,

"There is something you can do for me. Can you provide me with a spool of thin copper wire?"

"Of course, Dweller Jett. How much copper wire will you require?"

"13.5 meters."

"13.5 meters of copper wire. As you wish."

No sooner had Bob repeated the request than did exactly 13.5 meters of thin copper wire appear at the foot of Jett's bed.

"Excellent," Jett declared. "Can I also have an iTouch?"

"Yes, Dweller Jett, you may have an iTouch."

The iTouch too appeared as requested. Encouraged by this development, Jett requested each of the parts necessary to build a new quantum swapper. Bob never once inquired as to the purpose of the items but furnished them as requested without protest.

"Will there be anything else, Dweller Jett?"

"Yes, I'd like an ice cold Dr. Pepper and some privacy."

"Of course, Dweller Jett."

The drink appeared on the table where Jett had assembled his horde of tools and parts.

"I am programmed to please, happy tinkering," Bob stated and Jett heard what sounded like a computer powering off.

Jett grabbed his soda from the table and took several long deep gulps. He placed the empty can down and turned his attention to the parts sprawled out before him. He picked up the copper wire and bent it into the shape of a double helix. Jett became fully absorbed in his work, so much so that he didn't notice the hours as they passed. In time, he cobbled together a perfect replica of his original machine.

"Now all I need is some bearing as to where I am and a way to power up."

Jett looked around his room. He noticed his laptop open on his desk. Jett walked over to it and pressed the space bar. The laptop turned on as it normally would only the interface wasn't that of the computer he recognized. On the screen was a simple question: What would you like to know?

Jett typed: Where is Oonuua?

The computer replied, "Oonuua is the seat of The Fold. It is located on the fourth planet of the Aaptuuan System in the spiral galaxy of Caslu." A three dimensional hologram of the galaxy appeared over the keyboard with the Aaptuuan system highlighted in yellow.

Then Jett typed: Where is Earth?

The computer replied, "No file found for Earth."

Jett thought for a moment and said, "Of course..." and then typed: Where is Solaris 3?

A hologram appeared and rotated until it highlighted a red system on the edge of one of the galaxy's spiral arms. Jett examined the hologram intensely. He knew if he could calculate the distance and direction, he could theoretically make his way home and warn the people of Earth.

Jett typed: What is the distance between Oonuua and San Jose, California?

The computer responded: "3.524 hours' time."

Jett had never contemplated traveling such a distance with his device. He was ecstatic when he was able to move a Lego across his bedroom, but based on everything he read in his mom's papers, distance was irrelevant in the space between space. Then Jett wondered, "If they can read my mind, then they must know what I'm up to." Silence.

"They must know," Jett paused, "...what I'm up to." Silence.

"Room... err, Bob?" Jett said.

"Yes, Dweller Jett. Do you again require my assistance?" Bob asked.

"Yes, Bob. What did I make with the stuff you gave me?"

"I would not know, Dweller Jett. I am programed to fulfill your desires. What I am able to provide you is based upon your access level. What you have requested thus far is authorized. What you do with it is of little concern to me."

"What is not authorized?" Jett asked curiously.

"I will not know until you make a request I cannot fulfill," Bob answered.

"Can I have a bazooka?"

"No, Dweller Jett," Bob replied, "You may not have a bazooka."

"Can I have a ship to get out of here?"

"No," Bob replied, "but you may have the simulation of doing so."

"Not quite the same is it?"

"You would be unable to tell the difference," Bob responded.

Jett smirked. "May I have an Aaptuuan battery pack?"

Bob was silent for a moment or two and finally said, "Yes, you may have a quantum energy storage cylinder."

"A what?"

"A battery, Dweller Jett, the best reference I have for

your request is a quantum energy storage cylinder. Is this what you desire?"

"Yes," Jett replied expectantly.

"You are authorized to receive a maximum Level 2 power output. Will that meet your requirements?"

Jett had no idea what 'Level 2' power output meant and simply said that it would be sufficient, and as with everything else Jett requested, the battery appeared on the table before him. Jett painstakingly integrated the alien battery into his device. He turned his attention to the algorithm that swapped matter from one place to another. He did not wish to again be swapped to some high altitude only to plummet to his death this time or suddenly appear in the vacuum of space where he stood no chance of survival, or worse to end up in the middle of a rock somewhere.

Therefore, he made several adjustments that would account for such contingencies. First, he needed to account for breathable air, next for gravity, and last for the density of positive matter and his proximity to it. The Aaptuuans' computer databases gave him information scarcely imaginable on Earth and it allowed him to fine tune his invention with meticulous precision on a galactic scale creating a four dimensional intergalactic GPS.

One of the major advancements involved sending a small sensor ahead of the soon to-be swapped payload. The sensor was designed to determine if the destination fit the criteria provided. If the location was deemed inhospitable, the jump would abort. Lastly, Jett made a final tweak that allowed for multiple 'safe swap' calculations to be made simultaneously so that if an emergency swap was required, the computer would select the safest choice. Jett just needed to test his newly revamped machine.

He knew that if he activated his machine, it would attract the attention of the Aaptuuans. In fact, he was quite surprised no one had intervened so far. Were they not watching him at all? Did they feel he stood no chance of escape or was this his path? Did they actually want him to escape for some reason? It didn't really matter to him so long as he was able to make it home and warn humanity of its impending fate.

Jett approached the computer terminal and typed, where is Le-Wa?

The computer offered hundreds of simultaneous locations on several planets.

"Ok," Jett thought, "this is a problem." He turned away from the terminal and asked Bob, "Bob, where are the two Aaptuuans who escorted me to see The Council?"

"They are preparing to leave on a mission to the Ciallorean System," Bob replied, "They are on Landing Platform A-437-DDJ68."

"Thank you, Bob," Jett said graciously as he entered the landing platform information into his device's newly updated galactic positioning system - courtesy of the Aaptuuan interstellar mapping project.

"Why do you require such information, Dweller Jett?"

"I plan to join them momentarily," Jett answered.

"That will be quite impossible, Dweller Jett, but they will visit you when they return from their mission. They have already booked an appointment to do so in three weeks' time. They are both quite fond of you."

"I'm afraid I'm going to need to reschedule that

appointment, Bob."

"Of course, Dweller Jett. What time would you prefer the appointment," Bob requested.

"I would like to see them... Now!" Jett smiled as he initiated the swap sequence and disappeared in a flash.

"Appointment rescheduled and confirmed," Bob replied. Then Bob continued, "Dweller Jett Joseph Javelin Junior quantum jump completed 13.98827 cycles ahead of schedule. His quantum energy cylinder will allow for one additional quantum jump."

A hologram appeared in Jett's room. It was Dr. VaaCaam-a.

"Jett's tracking chip has been activated. Monitor Dweller Jett's movements and report any subsequent jumps to The Council."

"As you wish, Dr. VaaCaam-a," Bob replied.

VaaCaam-a's hologram then paced slowly through Jett's room and out onto the terrace.

"May The Great White Light guide you, Jett," he said spreading his arms out to the Oonuuan skyline.

Chapter 9
Shift into Neutral

Jett reappeared wedged tightly between two large cargo containers.

"Well, I guess the swapper works, even if only slightly better than finding myself inside of one of these boxes," Jett muttered as he attempted to wiggle himself free.

It took some doing, but Jett finally managed to pop himself out. He looked around. He was in a cavernous cargo hanger. It was lined with large cube-shaped containers organized in long rows. The walls sported displays of diagrams and scrolling symbols he did not understand. There were no visible doors but he noticed a number of portholes. He crept over to the nearest of these and peaked outside. Beneath him was the landing platform and in the distance he saw the Oonuuan skyline.

"This must be Le-Wa's ship," he said to himself before being thrown backward into one of the containers by a sudden jolt. The spacecraft shot off of the platform and straight into the sky. Jett sunk in the floor up to his knees.

"Oh no, not this weird metal again," he complained, "I can't pull my feet out. It's like quicksand."

Jett looked around the hold and noticed that all of the white boxes had sunk into the floor by an equal amount. Then he remembered his trip to Aaptuu 4. He knew that he was about to become encased in the metal.

"Oh crap. I better relax," he reassured himself remembering Le-Wa's advice.

The craft accelerated. The quasi-liquid metal crept

higher up his legs. He could feel it pass his pelvis and engulf his bellybutton. As it moved higher up his body, Jett looked around and noticed the ceiling closing in on him. He looked out the window and saw Aaptuu 4 as it receded rapidly into the distance. The light of passing stars grew into millions of long thin threads and connected to one another. The porthole window disappeared. Jett took a deep breath and shut his eyes as the metal enveloped him.

The sensation was at once both frightening and exhilarating. The experience would best be compared to riding an extreme roller coaster in your sleeping bag while wearing a blindfold. At least that's how Jett would describe it later to his family.

Unfortunately this time around, Jett was not seated as optimally as he was on his trip to Aaptuu 4, and it was every bit as uncomfortable as Le-Wa warned, yet the trip itself was over in a relatively short time as far as Jett could reckon. He felt the metal pull slowly away, and as the last of it left his body, he collapsed to the floor.

"I feel awful," he moaned, "I don't think this gets easier with practice," he complained as he awkwardly rose to his knees, shook his head, and painfully stood up.

The porthole windows reappeared along with the giant white boxes and computer screens. Jett brought his face close to one of the windows and looked outside. Outside was a greenish yellow planet surrounded by several moons. On its dark side, the lights of a thousand cities twinkled. More lights sparkled on each of the moons and in between floated dozens of large space stations.

"Where am I?" he wondered.

Jett searched the swapper's galactic positioning database for his coordinates. The iTouch screen eventually displayed a very long number and the word, 'Ciallore.'

"Ciallore, that must be this planet," he deduced. The iTouch displayed a system with five planets. The second planet was highlighted.

"What are Le-Wa and Chi-Col doing here?" he wondered aloud.

Jett pressed on with his research. He learned that the Ciallore System was home to a very intelligent but ruthless species that inhabited Ciallore 2 and several of its moons. Cialloria Suprema began gathering in permanent settlements some 4,000 of their years ago. Today they were among the last surviving species on a planet that once hosted billions of life forms.

Cialloria Suprema has a lustful taste for flesh and finds virtually every organism palatable in one form or another. As a result, they devoured most of their planet's other species into extinction. Recently their scientists developed a worm hole drive that would allow them near unfettered access to the rest of the galaxy. In order to contain this scourge, The Fold ordered neutralization by way of Hyper-sine Interrupter Radiation or H.I.R.

"So that's why they're here," Jett thought. "How bad could this species be to deserve this? Who was The Fold to decide their fate? How was this ok in the eyes of The Ten Laws?"

Above him on the bridge Le-Wa and Chi-Col went somberly about their work.

"Finalizing trajectory and dispersement," Chi-Col

reported. "Full neutralization in 3.22 cycles. Clean up patrols in position."

"Commencing neutralization protocol," said Le-Wa, "in 3, 2, 1..."

Le-Wa waved his hand slightly above the command console and a series of white squares lit up in a holographic display. Below deck Jett heard a loud whooshing sound. He jumped to his feet and looked around wildly. A series of fiery orange lines appeared along the edges and down the center of the cargo hold.

Jett realized what has about to happen, "Oh my god, the cargo doors are opening into space. I'll be sucked out with everything else!" Jett grabbed the quantum swapper and ran outside the fiery orange oval as quickly as his feet would move. He looked for something to hold on to, but the hanger's smooth walls offered nothing.

Jett looked back toward the white boxes and slumped against the wall behind him. As he did, he felt himself sink ever so slightly into the wall. Jett turned and faced the featureless wall. He pulled up his sleeves and gently reached into the wall. The wall accepted his hands like a pair of well-worn gloves. He kept pushing until he'd gone just past his elbows, careful to wedge the swapper between himself and the wall. He gingerly pushed the tips of his shoes into the wall.

No sooner had he done this then the cargo doors swung open. Every one of the large containers dropped into the vacuum of space. Jett was pulled violently toward the door, but his arms and feet were secured snugly in the metal wall. When the cargo bay doors finally closed, Jett slammed violently into the wall and slowly pulled his feet and arms out. With the exception of Jett and the quantum swapper, the cargo hold was now completely empty, and he again turned his attention to what was happening outside.

The white containers formed a 'V' like formation as they flew toward Ciallore 2.

Ciallorean ships in the vicinity opened fire on the cubes with a volley of missiles and other projectiles. The salvo did nothing to stop the cube formation, but the Cialloreans were not deterred. They launched a second attack, but it too proved fruitless as their munitions deflected harmlessly off an invisible energy field.

After a few more unsuccessful attacks, the Ciallorean warships gave the white containers a wide berth, tracking them at a distance as the formation positioned itself above the planet's North Pole.

The containers split into several groups. One contingent surrounded the planet, and the others surrounded the moons. Ciallorean ships shadowed each group. Every now and again they fired provocatively at the white cubes, but all attempts at deterring the containers were unsuccessful.

Once in position, the containers began to spin and blink in unison. This development agitated the Cialloreans and they launched a massive assault on the alien objects.

Jett watched the exchange curiously. He noticed the ships nearest the spinning objects suddenly lose power and begin to float aimlessly in space. They slammed violently into each other.

Blackouts followed on the dark sides of Ciallore 2 and its moons. Jett watched as all of the lights went out. The last objects to lose power were the orbiting space stations.

"So this is neutralization," Jett said, "They just turn off the lights."

Jett thought about Earth and what a permanent loss of power would mean for his species and his planet. His face fired red with rage.

"They can't do that to us! We haven't done anything to deserve this!"

Jett was beside himself. Would humanity's blood be on his hands? Did he single handedly bring about Armageddon? Jett watched as the powerless spacecraft smashed into each other and exploded. He observed in horror as hundreds of ships burned up in Ciallore 2's atmosphere as they rained down on the planet's surface.

"All of this death," he said, "How can the Aaptuuans do this to them? I can't let them do this to Earth."

Jett searched the interstellar mapping database for the coordinates of Solaris 3 and his room in San Jose, California, but before he could finish a door opened in the wall of the cargo hold. Le-Wa appeared.

"Jett," Le-Wa telepathed, "What are you doing here?"

"You destroyed their whole civilization," Jett replied.

"Yes, it is unfortunate, but necessary."

"Necessary? Necessary to kill all of those beings?"

"Necessary to protect the innocents of the galaxy whom the Cialloreans would kill without warning or remorse and serve up as culinary curiosities," Le-Wa replied.

"How do you know for sure they'd kill anyone much less eat them?"

"We've observed Ciallore 2 for over 10,000 of your years. They have annihilated virtually every species they have come in contact with. The only ones they have not exterminated, subsist in brutal conditions as food. You, Jett, would be a holiday buffet for them."

"And you will do the same to my people?"

"We hope to avoid that, Jett, but if your invention proliferates, we would have no choice. The Solarians' flesh lust is not so unlike that of the Cialloreans."

"I won't let you do it!" Jett shouted as he fiddled with the quantum swapper distractedly. "And I'll get there before you."

"Jett, there is no need to fear us. We want to help you."

"Did you try to help the Cialloreans?"

"There was no hope for them."

Jett made a couple of adjustments. He turned a knob and entered something into the iTouch.

"Sayonara suckers!" Jett announced as he activated his device and disappeared into the space between space.

Le-Wa stood there quietly for a moment. "Jett has made his second jump."

"Tracking," said Bob, "I will let you know where and when Dweller Jett arrives on Solaris 3."

There was a long pause.

"Well," Le-Wa asked, "Jett should be there by now. Can you see him?"

Another long pause ensued and then Bob replied, "There seems to be a problem..."

Chapter 10
A Slight Miscalculation

When Jett opened his eyes, the cargo hold was gone, and he found himself in a vast barren desert.

"I must have mixed up the coordinates," Jett said, "but at least I'm back on Earth."

Jett looked around. There were tall flat mesas and bluffs all around him. They were comprised of red and brown sedimentary rock. Red and gray boulders of all sizes lay strewn about as far as his eyes could see. Jett didn't see any plants or a single cloud in the sky.

"This must be Arizona or New Mexico, or something in the American Southwest. Hopefully I'm not stranded in the middle of Death Valley. Just need to check my iTouch and I'll..."

Jett looked down at his machine. The iTouch screen was black.

"Probably need to reboot it," he muttered and proceeded to try every button combination he knew or could think of. Still, nothing happened. The iTouch was dead.

"Guess I better start walking and try to find some help."

Jett turned in a circle, but didn't see any signs of civilization. There were no roads, no paths, no sign that people had ever visited this desolate stretch of nothingness. He had no bearing, even the sun seemed to be in the wrong place in the sky.

"I can't tell which way is north. I'll need to get up high so I can get a look around. Let's see..." he thought and climbed up the nearest large boulder. From his new vantage point, he could see just how in the middle of nowhere he was. Jett spotted a climbable mesa that was relatively close by. He jumped down from the boulder and began walking briskly toward it.

This desert was strangely empty to him. There were no plants, and for such a sunny day it was unexpectedly chilly. Jett didn't hear any sounds other than those of his own footsteps and breath. The air itself was unusually dry and Jett quickly became parched. Then he heard a rumbling in the distance.

He stopped and listened intently. Whatever it was appeared to be heading in his direction, but he couldn't identify it. It sounded like lots of basketballs bouncing simultaneously. Jett climbed up on the nearest boulder and looked in the direction of the growing racket. He saw a cloud of red dust rising up between boulders in the distance. The mysterious noise raced directly toward him.

"It doesn't sound like trucks or quads or cows..." Jett listened some more, "No, it's definitely balls bouncing. Lots and lots of them."

He turned his eyes toward the horizon and saw dozens of red balls bouncing up and down between the rocks.

"What the...?" he asked himself nervously as he squatted down on the boulder and tried to stay out of sight. Jett remembered his machine and jumped down from the boulder to retrieve it. There on the ground next to it was a red ball. It looked like the type of ball you'd use in gym class except this one had a long deep uneven line down one side of it. Jett grabbed the swapper and slowly backed away. As he did, it rolled toward him.

Jett stopped. It stopped. Jett slowly backed up. The ball

slowly rolled toward him. Jett turned and ran and it chased him. It was soon joined by a dozen others. Jett didn't understand what was going on. He thought that maybe he had swapped himself right into Area 51 and that these balls were experimental drones bent on his destruction.

An ever increasing army of them bounced along both sides of him. They flanked him and encircled him. Jett's escape route was cut off. He skidded to a halt.

"Oh, crap…"

The balls remained frozen. They sat perfectly still, waiting.

Jett wondered who made these things and what they were for. Were they robots? Were they remote controlled? Why were there so many different sizes?

He cautiously approached one of the smallest ones and squatted down next to it to examine every detail. As he got closer he noticed the outer shell, while appearing smooth from a distance, was covered with small dimples like those on an orange. Other than the uneven black jagged line along one side of it, the ball had no other discernible features.

Jett reached down and picked it up.

"It's warm," he observed, "and I think it's breathing."

He held the ball up and stared at it in amazement. He focused on the jagged black line. It was approximately half the diameter of the ball and charcoal in color. It was lined with deep uneven creases.

"What the heck is this thing?" he said rotating it in his hands.

The jagged line split open and became a mouth filled with sharp black teeth, blue gums, and a long black tongue. Jett dropped the ball in horror and backed into a tall boulder. The ball bounced harmlessly on the ground and rolled to a stop a few feet away. The black line closed, and Jett wondered if he had imagined the whole thing.

"I must be losing my mind," Jett gasped, "All this swapping and hyperspace travel must be getting to me."

He looked at the dozens of other balls surrounding him. They hadn't moved so much as a millimeter. Jett shrugged his shoulders. He picked up his machine and resumed his journey to the low mesa. No sooner had he taken his first step than did the balls converge on him.

Jett stopped, but this time the balls continued to roll toward him. They stopped suddenly a few centimeters away and one by one opened their mouths until all bared their sharp black teeth. The little one he had dropped rolled up to the front and stopped just before Jett's feet. The black line turned up toward Jett, opened hungrily, and lunged at him!

Jett covered his face with his forearms anticipating the ball would slam into him teeth first, but nothing happened. After a few seconds, Jett peaked out. The ball had vanished. Even stranger, the remaining balls slowly rolled away from him. Jett stepped toward the balls threateningly and they all jumped back. Jett hesitated a moment. When everything was perfectly still, he jumped forcefully and sent a cloud of red dust billowing up all around him. The balls sped off in every direction bouncing on, over, and through the boulders. They left a thick cloud of reddish dust in their wake.

"Ok, not quite sure what to make of that. Better get out of here before I run into any more surprises."

Jett again turned toward the low mesa and gasped.

Before him stood a large creature. It was at least seven feet tall with a squarish head sporting twelve squarish eyes. The sides of its body were covered with long rusty orange tentacles that stuck out of its silver metal suit like play dough pushed through a spaghetti press. In the center of the suit were four squares resembling a checkerboard. Each of its tentacles held a red ball. Jett stepped backwards and fell. He dropped his machine and it smashed on the rocks.

"Damn it!" Jett looked up at the creature and continued, "Nice giant grotesque monster. My name is Jett. I mean you no harm. Also, ummmm, you should know that I don't taste very good; nothing but skin and bones and a ton of processed food. Really bad stuff," he said nervously.

The creature didn't respond.

"So if you're not going to eat me, I'm just gonna get going," Jett said motioning toward the horizon.

The checkerboard in the center of its chest opened and a large parrot like beak emerged. The creature unceremoniously tossed one of the red balls into its beak and crunched down on it making a disgusting pop. The remaining balls wailed out in panic and squirmed furiously in the creature's tentacles as they desperately tried to escape. The creature proceeded to eat the balls one after the other in rapid succession until the last wailing ball was silenced with a gruesome pop. Dark black liquid coursed down the creature's silver suit.

"Ummm, like I said before, I don't taste very good. Nowhere near as tasty as those red balls. That's for sure! In fact, I have a great idea... Why don't we play hide and seek. You go over there," Jett suggested pointing at a large rock, "and count to a million. I'll just hide somewhere and when you're, um, done, you can come and find me, or perhaps you could find some more of those yummy little guys? C'mon, what do you say?"

The creature stood there silently. It slowly cocked its head to one side.

"Well?" Jett coaxed.

The creature didn't move.

"Ok," Jett said tentatively, "If you don't mind, I'll just gather up my things and get on my way."

Jett picked up his broken quantum swapper. The iTouch was smashed and several of the tubes bent or broken.

"It's going to be impossible to fix this thing," he cussed under his breath. Jett turned back to the creature, "Yeah so, see you later and stuff."

As Jett turned away, the creature pursued him with blinding speed and grabbed him in its tentacles. It pulled him up toward its checkerboard chest plate. The center opened and an octopus like beak emerged. Everything went black.

Chapter II
Stranger in a Strange Land

Jett opened his eyes to a dim room. He was lying on a deep crypt-like shelf carved into the rock. As he came to his senses, his eyes focused on a lantern whose light cast long shadows about the floor. Jett sat up and gathered himself.

He found himself in a cave with no windows. There was a single arched door that led to another cavern just beyond his view. An enormous shadow moved about in that room. It paced back and forth impatiently, breathing deeply as it went.

The memory of the creature rushed back. It must have taken him back to its lair.

"It hasn't eaten me yet. I'll take that as positive," Jett muttered to himself.

Jett's eyes adjusted to the light. The walls were awash in beautiful murals of the desert outside. Ledges were lined with sculptures. He stood up and quietly crept over to one of them nearby. The piece was a long vertical 'U' stretched out like a ribbon of taffy, fat at both ends but thin in the middle where the two ends met the base.

This specific portion of the sculpture seemed impossibly thin, in fact, and didn't look anywhere near strong enough to support the two much larger ends. Jett reached out and carefully picked it up. The sculpture was much lighter than he expected. For its size, roughly a meter and a half tall, Jett would've guessed it weighed five to seven kilos, but it was much closer to two kilos, maybe even less. He placed it back down and picked up another. As Jett lifted it, the piece knocked several other sculptures to the floor with a deafening crash.

The enormous shadow in the other room froze in its tracks. Jett attempted to put the sculpture back on the ledge but in his nervous haste, he missed and it too crashed to the floor.

"Oh, geez..." Jett murmured.

The giant shadow lumbered to the archway with heavy steps.

"Ummm, hello?" Jett quivered, "I'm really glad you haven't eaten me. Ummm, thanks for bringing me back here - wherever here is," Jett continued, "and away from those crazy ball creatures..."

The creature entered the cavern and approached him. "Ummm, I don't want any trouble, errr, sir. I'm just looking to get home. Seems like I may have swapped myself to the wrong planet, ha ha ha," Jett laughed nervously.

The creature paused for a moment and cocked its square head to one side. Jett swallowed hard and waited. He figured that if the creature had intended to eat him, it would've done so already or at the very least locked him up somewhere for safe keeping.

Judging from the quality of the sculptures and cave paintings, this creature was highly intelligent and maybe even civilized. Was it possible this thing might possess the technology necessary to fix his quantum swapper?

The creature carefully approached Jett so as not to startle or frighten him. It stopped in front of him and held its six tentacles out to the side before wrapping all but one behind itself. This last tentacle snaked its way to just millimeters from Jett's nose. Cross-eyed, Jett noticed a smallish brown hook on the end of it.

The hook moved up and touched his forehead. He felt

a mild electrical tingle. It didn't hurt, it just sort of tickled a bit. Then Jett saw a flash. Instantly, he found himself in a strange world. The experience was like watching an old black and white movie without sound. The city's sidewalks were crowded with creatures like the one that had brought him here. Strange vehicles moved up and down the streets and flew through the air above him. The buildings were tall with rounded tops and large oval windows.

The scene changed. It remained black and white, but now he saw strange creatures of all shapes and sizes. There were balls, similar to the ones that had chased him. There were giant worms, ten legged insects, and snake-like bird monsters straight out of his worst nightmare. Jett saw himself wandering through the desert, being chased by the balls, and ultimately confronting the creature who saved him. He saw himself faint.

The creature pulled its tentacle away from Jett's forehead and Jett snapped back to the dim reality of the cave.

"You're able to transmit your thoughts through that hook of yours?" Jett asked.

The creature didn't answer. It simply turned and left the room.

"Was it something I said?" Jett quipped.

Within a few moments, the creature returned with a plate of food and a cup full of liquid. It offered the fare to Jett.

"Are you sure I can eat this?" Jett asked, "It's not going to kill me is it?"

The creature handed the items to Jett and took a seat on the ledge opposite him.

"Ok," he said skeptically, "batten down the hatches, or whatever..."

Jett raised the glass to his lips. He was desperately thirsty, but before he sipped it, he took a long deliberate sniff. It smelled OK. It didn't smell like anything really. He tentatively took a sip. It was water.

"Water," Jett said chugging it down, "That's a relief. Now what's this other stuff?"

Jett placed the empty stone cup down and picked at his plate. He sniffed one item after another before he mustered the courage to nibble at what appeared to be a sliced red fruit. To his delight, it tasted like a sweet apple/carrot/potato if one can imagine such a thing. Next he nibbled at another mystery food. It tasted like an earthy beet/banana/garlic something or other.

Since he was hungry and the food didn't taste all that bad or appear to be toxic, he devoured it all. When he was finished, he placed the plate down on the ledge beside him and tried to anticipate the creature's next move.

A few very awkward and silent minutes passed before the creature stood up and walked over to Jett. As it did before, it held its tentacles out to its sides and rolled them all behind itself with the exception of the single hooked one. Jett closed his eyes, and the creature again placed the hook on Jett's forehead.

This time, though, the pictures were vividly full color. There were vast red deserts with wide canyons and tall desolate buttes. These gave way to a vast ocean teeming with strange and wonderful sea life. Soon he was soaring over coastal cliffs and snowcapped peaks. It was a whirlwind tour of the planet this creature called home, and it was most definitely *not* Earth.

"I'm not home, am I?"

"No," a deep slow voice vibrated in his mind.

"Where am I?"

"You are on Lanedaar 3," the voice replied.

"Where is that?"

"It's where you are."

"I mean where in the galaxy? Where is this planet in relation to my planet?"

"What is your planet called?"

"My planet is called Earth. You may know it as Solaris 3."

"I am sorry. I'm afraid I don't know it by either name. You are on Lanedaar 3. I am Tii-Eldii."

"Are you here all by yourself?"

"Yes. Quite," Tii-Eldii answered sadly.

"What were those red ball things that were chasing me?"

"Those were charlatones. They would have torn you to pieces had I not arrived when I did."

"You ate them..."

"Yes, but I did it more to make a point to the rest of the pack to scare them off. They don't taste very good and they give me terrible indigestion."

"Are there other creatures like the charlatones on this planet?"

"Yes. You are advised to stay close to me or remain in the cave at all times."

"I appreciate that, I truly do," Jett replied, "but I don't plan to stay very long. I'm going back to my planet as soon as I can fix this."

Jett walked over to his broken quantum swapper. He picked it up and brought it to Tii-Eldii. Tii-Eldii placed the hook on Jett's forehead.

"It's broken now and I'm not sure I can fix it. I need a new iTouch and some way to recharge the batteries. You don't happen to have an Amazon Local nearby, do you?"

"A what?"

"Never mind, you wouldn't understand."

"I might. You need to think about that place and I will see it."

Jett closed his eyes and concentrated on San Jose. He saw office parks full of tech companies. He envisioned the restaurants in downtown Palo Alto and the engineering lab where his mom worked at Stanford. Then he pictured himself at Amazon Local buying a new iTouch and a battery charger.

"I see," Tii-Eldii said, "Unfortunately, there is nothing like that on Lanedaar 3. Perhaps there is another way to fix it."

"I don't know," Jett said. "Looks like I'm stuck here for now. Meanwhile the Aaptuuans are going to neutralize my planet and it's all my fault. All because of my quantum swapper..."

"Aaptuuans?" Tii-Eldii asked.

"Yes. Aaptuuans. Do you know them?"

"I do. They are the reason I'm here. Tell me, why are the Aaptuuans interested in your planet?"

"They say my invention makes the human race a threat to galactic peace. They keep talking about these ten laws and this fold thing. They took me to their planet and put me in a room named Bob, and..."

Tii-Eldii straightened up and raced out of the room.

"Where are you going?" Jett called after him.

Tii-Eldii returned in a flash. He placed his hook on Jett's head. In a second tentacle he held a long silver wand.

"The Aaptuuans will track you here if they haven't already," Tii-Eldii said nervously, "I need to remove your chip."

"Chip?"

Tii-Eldii slowly scanned Jett's body with the wand. Half way down Jett's left arm it flashed red.

"There it is. Now hold still or it will get away," Tii-Eldii said impatiently as he brought around a third tentacle that held a sharp syringe.

Petrified, Jett watched Tii-Eldii get to work. The syringe shot a beam of light into Jett's arm and a small lump began racing up his bicep, but just before it reached his shoulder the light drew it out.

"Here it is," Tii-Eldii said holding up a small grey capsule, "Now I must destroy it."

Tii-Eldii produced a jar of clear liquid. He dropped the capsule into the liquid and it bubbled and foamed up violently. The liquid again turned calm and clear. The capsule was gone.

"Do you think they, ummm, know where I am?"

"Yes, Jett, there is a high probability they know you are here. They will find me as well. My days of hiding have come to an end after all these long years."

"Why do you care if the Aaptuuans find you? They're peaceful and you've done nothing wrong... have you?"

"The Aaptuuans would love to find me. I escaped from them long ago."

"You mean..."

"Yes, Jett. Fate has brought us together though I do not

yet understand why," Tii-Eldii reflected as he stood up to leave.

"Where are you going?"

"We must hurry. The Aaptuuans will arrive soon."

Chapter 12
The Search for Jett

The Aaptuuan craft decelerated as it approached the outer edge of the remote eight planet system. The metal cocoons withdrew, morphing into matching silver captain's chairs.

"Calculating final approach trajectory," Le-Wa reported.

"We will reach our destination in 3.223 cycles," Chi-Col responded, "tracking chip activated."

The ship maneuvered gracefully through the system's outer planets and asteroid belt. In the distance they saw a fragile blue planet.

"Solaris 3 in range. Moon station time of arrival - 0.22 cycles."

They approached the moon in a long arc and landed in a crater ringed with dusty hatches and small buildings on the dark side.

"No response from Jett's tracker, chip signal amplified," Chi-Col said as he waved his hands over various holographic screens. After a few moments Chi-Col continued, "I am not picking up any transmissions from Solaris 3. It is possible he did not jump here."

"Yes, but protocol dictates that we must make a physical check of the surface. Jett's chip may have been compromised as a result of his multiple exchanges. We will begin our sweep on the dark side of the planet."

The Aaptuuan ship left the moon's surface and sped toward Solaris 3. The continents on the dark side of the planet were defined by billions of twinkling lights.

"Biometric matching sequence initiated," Le-Wa reported.

Biometric matching technology allowed the Aaptuuans to find their wards in the event of a tracking chip malfunction. The technology was designed to map an individual organism's biometric makeup and brain wave patterns. Remarkably, in a boundless universe, no two known organisms shared exact biometric patterns. This was true even among individual members of the same species including identical twins. It was an interstellar fingerprint of sorts.

Holographic images depicted outlines of human shapes and color coded data in rapid succession. Le-Wa guided the ship down into the troposphere above equatorial Africa.

"Cloak activated. Geostationary position established. Now we will wait," he said.

The hours ticked off slowly as the Earth passed gradually beneath them. The Aaptuuans waded patiently through mountains of data. The continental outlines of Africa and Europe became the blackness of the Atlantic Ocean which itself yielded to the Lite-Brite outline of the Americas. So far their search had turned up only a few quasi matches, those of Jett's distant relatives, most of whom he had never met.

"Jett's home settlement approaching. Moving geostationary position to the northern hemisphere."

Le-Wa guided their ship north over Central America and along the dim outline of sparsely settled Baja California. Soon the bright lights of Los Angeles and coastal California shined below. The biometric scans continued in earnest, but there was no sign of Jett.

"It is becoming increasingly likely that Jett did not jump home. It is possible he accidentally jumped somewhere else or was himself destroyed in transit."

"We will interrogate those most likely to have had contact with Jett before completing our sweep."

The Aaptuuan ship guided itself silently toward Jett's family home. The holographic scans detected Jett's parents and brother, Jack. One of the scans grew larger than the rest and flashed prominently.

"We will question Jett's mother. Locking in on her pattern now," Le-Wa stated.

Evelyn sat at her desk in the Stanford engineering lab. She was perplexed by her son's blue prints. She and her engineering students had constructed a device similar to the one called out by the plans and demonstrated in the video Jack gave her, but they had no luck actually getting it to work.

Evelyn closed her laptop and turned off the reading lamp on her desk. She leaned back in her chair, took off her glasses, and gently rubbed her eyes. It had been another long frustrating day at the lab. She looked forward to a good night's sleep and a fresh start in the morning.

Evelyn stood up and left her office. She walked down the dimly lit hallway to the nearest exit. The door slammed hard behind her. At 11:45pm there were few cars remaining in the faculty lot. Her white BMW was parked under a solitary flickering street light.

Keys jingling in her hand, Evelyn hustled to her parking spot. She had never felt unsafe on campus before, but tonight she had an uneasy feeling and she looked about nervously, keeping one hand on the small can of Mace in her purse. She scanned the parking lot for the ever present campus security, but she saw no one. When she arrived at her car, she opened the driver's door and tossed her bag inside, but as Evelyn lifted her foot to get in, she was engulfed in a white light.

There was a blinding flash and Evelyn found herself standing in a brightly lit silver metal chamber with no windows, doors, ceilings, or floors. A chair rose up out of the nothingness in front of her.

"Please have a seat," an angelic voice urged.

"Who are you?" Evelyn demanded. "Why have you brought me here? What do you want from me?"

"We would very much like to help you find your son, Jett. Can you help us do that?" the hypnotic voice asked.

"Jett? What do you want with Jett?"

"Please be seated, Evelyn. Our intent is to ensure Jett's safe return home. You also want that for Jett, do you not?"

The narcotic voice calmed Evelyn. She felt drowsy. "OK, I'll sit down."

"Good," the voice reassured, "now close your eyes... relax... drift away..."

Evelyn obediently followed the instructions and was soon deeply hypnotized. Her chair slowly morphed into an examination table and Le-Wa entered the chamber. He approached Evelyn. He visually examined her before placing a finger on each of her temples.

Le-Wa accessed Evelyn's most recent memories. She labored to recreate Jett's device in her laboratory. She reviewed his designs and brilliantly creative algorithms. She and her team were getting close. Le-Wa saw trips to the Farmer's Market and a lot of family discussion related to Jett's disappearance. Evelyn cried a lot. She missed her son terribly and was determined to find him. Evelyn had not seen Jett since he vanished.

"Le-Wa," Chi-Col telepathed, "Incoming transmission from Aaptuu 4. Stand-by..."

A screen appeared on the wall, it was Dr. VaaCaam-a. "We have received a signal from Jett's tracking chip. The transmission was brief, but we were able to determine that Jett is in the Lanedaar System. Lanedaar is Solaris' twin in the Shoolan sector. Jett's condition is uncertain. According to our records, intelligence on Lanedaar 3 is primitive with the notable exception of large worms living beneath the planet's crust. The surface itself is hostile and wrought with calamity. You will go there immediately. Jett's fate must be determined."

The transmission ended. Le-Wa waved his hand and the examination table changed into a driver's seat. There was a flash of light and Evelyn found herself sitting at the wheel of her car. The Bimmer's door chime chirped at her.

"I'm working way too hard," she said shaking her head and rubbing her temples. She shut the car door and drove away into the night.

Suspended just a few meters in the sky above her, Le-Wa and Chi-Col busied themselves for the next leg of their mission.

"Lanedaar 3 is a very dangerous place for a Solarian organism of Jett's design," Le-Wa observed, "I participated in one of the first explorations of the Lanedaar System. It is the primary reason I was assigned to Solaris. The systems are remarkably similar, near twins in fact. One startling similarity is the variety and voracity of the carnivores roaming the third

80

planet."

"I am certain we will locate him," Chi-Col responded. "It is imperative we do so soon. The fate of his planet hangs in the balance."

Chapter 13
Futile Flight

Tii-Eldii raced around his labyrinth of tunnels, and powered down every device that might use the faintest trace of electricity. He gathered supplies and stuffed them into large sacks. Between errands, he ran back and forth to the cave's mouth and gazed intently into the sky. Tii-Eldii's hustle and bustle gave Jett an uneasy feeling. It seemed that this creature, for reasons yet unknown, was genuinely frightened by the prospect of the Aaptuuans visiting his planet.

"Hey, let me give you a hand," Jett offered as he absentmindedly picked up a furry orange ball and tossed it up and down into the air. Eight spider-like eyes opened and glared at Jett.

"Ahhhh! What is that?" Jett exclaimed and he dropped the ball on the ground. It closed its eyes and rolled out of the room. Tii-Eldii let out a low deep laugh. Jett looked up at him.

"What's so funny?"

Tii-Eldii held his claw to Jett's forehead and said, "That is Nukii. She is my friend and companion. Several years ago, I stumbled upon her in the desert - kind of like you."

"It's one of those bouncing menaces that tried to eat me outside isn't it?"

"No. Not quite," Tii-Eldii replied, "She is a Lanedaarian bush bunny. She is quite tame, and, it appears, quite frightened of visitors. Don't worry, she'll warm up to you. Bush bunnies are quite intuitive, you know. They are a distant plant eating relative of the charlatone - the bouncing menaces you refer to. Bush bunnies survive on moss, lichen, and just about any type of plant material. In fact, Nukii here ate a good number of my cloth linens after I first brought her home. If I were you, I'd keep a close eye on your clothing.

"Evolving on this harsh world near the bottom of the food chain has given bush bunnies some interesting survival traits that include being born pregnant and having an uncanny ability to anticipate danger."

"You mean they can predict the future?"

"Well, they can anticipate events moments before they happen," Tii-Eldii emphasized.

"What's the difference?"

"Bush bunnies like Nukii have developed a neural system that causes their reflexes to act immediately *before* a life threatening event, say a charlatone ambush or a dive bombing Gull Snake."

"Gull snake," Jett murmured, "I don't think I want to bump into one of those."

"No, Jett, you would not and I would not wish it upon you. They are vile creatures, disgusting, and ever hungry. Gull snakes consume their prey slowly. Their saliva cauterizes their victim's wounds with every bite. Depending on the size of the prey, the dining process might take several agonizing weeks."

"Why do they eat so slowly?"

"Food is very scarce on Lanedaar's surface and what little there is to eat is very hard to catch. Theirs is a highly evolved survival strategy that is combined with an efficient metabolism designed to maximize the energy harvest of every meal. Keeping their prey alive prevents spoilage. Gull snake lairs are immaculately clean since there is no waste."

"They never go number one or number two?"

"I believe you mean to say the never urinate or defecate. Is that correct?"

"Umm, sure, whatever," Jett replied.

"As I said, there is no waste, every molecule of energy is harvested. Now I must return to my tasks. We cannot be too careful. The Aaptuuans will scan this entire planet in earnest if they believe you to be here. They will not stop until they find you."

"Are we leaving?" Jett asked.

"There is no leaving. There is only hiding. Come now, help me bring these bags to the back entrance."

Tii-Eldii picked up several of the large bags and lumbered through the archway. Once through, he turned his head and waved for Jett to join him. Jett shrugged his shoulders and bent down to pick up a bag.

"Grrrrr," Jett growled as he hoisted the bag up to his chest. With his back arched and straining under the load, Jett followed Tii-Eldii into the next cavern and through several others until they finally reached their destination. Jett dropped his heavy load onto the floor.

"Finally! What's back here anyway?" Jett asked exasperated.

"It's our way out. If we are to elude the Aaptuuans, we must go deeper into the planet's crust. In contrast to its harsh surface, Lanedaar's subsurface is rich with life, radioactivity, and magnetism. All this noise will disguise our biorhythms. Quickly now, there is more to do."

Tii-Eldii raced to the front chambers calling to Jett in a strange guttural voice as he went. Jett reluctantly followed Tii-Eldii.

"I don't know if I'm cut out for this kind of work," Jett said before he followed Tii-Eldii, "I should probably just let the Aaptuuans catch me. They're really not all that bad, you know. I could get used to Bob."

When Jett caught up, Tii-Eldii had his head stuck outside the door. He hovered there for a while.

"Are they here?" Jett asked.

Tii-Eldii waved one of his tentacles as if to say no. Then he came back into the cave and continued packing his things.

"If I can fix my machine," Jett suggested, "I can get us both out of here. I can take you home first and then go home myself. Do you have anything like this?" Jett asked as he lifted his machine off of the shelf and pointed at the iTouch and various other components.

Tii-Eldii looked at Jett and cocked his head slightly to the side.

"Do you?" Jett insisted. "I mean it. I can get us out of here, and now that you've disabled my tracking chip, there's no way they can find us."

Tii-Eldii approached Jett and placed his claw on his head, "Jett, we're not even sure if the Aaptuuans will come here looking for you. There is a chance I destroyed the chip before they received the transmission. It's possible I have some items that will allow you to repair your machine, but I do not have them here."

"You don't have them here? Where might you have them?"

"Deep in the planet's crust there is an empty magma chamber. This is where I have hidden the last of my people's technology. It is possible you will find what you need there, but first we must remove every trace of our presence in these caverns," Tii-Eldii insisted filling sack after sack.

"Why are you so afraid of them?" Jett asked.

Tii-Eldii shrugged and continued to work with blinding speed. Once he'd filled a half dozen sacks, he motioned to Jett to carry the one closest to him. Tii-Eldii effortlessly picked up the other five sacks and raced to the rear cave.

Jett picked up the remaining sack, which also happened to be the smallest, and followed Tii-Eldii down the dark and winding passage. In the corner of his eye, he saw Nukii tracking him from the dark crevices. Jett stopped. Nukii stopped. Jett took a couple of steps forward and Nukii followed suit. Nukii mirrored Jett's every move.

"Doesn't look like you're a too distant relative of those nasty charlatones. You both have the same annoying habits," Jett commented. Nukii purred softly. She then rolled over behind Jett and followed a meter or so behind.

"You're a curious little fellow aren't you? You'd be a big hit back home, especially with the ladies. They love cute little fur balls like you."

Soon Jett and Nukii caught up with Tii-Eldii. Jett tossed his sack on the pile with the others.

"How are we supposed to carry all of this stuff *and* run from the Aaptuuans? Couldn't you travel just a little bit lighter?"

Tii-Eldii laced his claw on Jett's head, "We will not carry it. Help will arrive shortly."

"Help?" Jett inquired.

"Yes. They will be here soon."

"...but I thought you were alone."

"I am, well except for Nukii. These helpers aren't very good company, but they are very good at carrying lots of stuff. Additionally, they won't eat us or be eaten by anything else in transit. Come, let's continue."

Nukii chirped furiously. Tii-Eldii turned toward the cave entrance. "We have company," he said.

"Aaptuuans?"

"Not sure, but something is coming," Tii-Eldii cautioned as he raced to the front. Jett sprinted behind him, but Tii-Eldii moved so quickly, Jett couldn't keep up.

When Tii-Eldii arrived at the mouth of the cave, he again peered into the sky. This time Tii-Eldii ducked his head back into the cave almost as soon as he stuck it out. He paced around nervously for a few seconds. Then he reached up and with amazing ease pulled a large boulder down in front of the cave's entrance. It smashed to the ground sending red dust up in a thick cloud.

"We have to go now. We must hide deep in the planet's crust. If we don't, they will capture us both and there is no telling what they will do with us then."

"You think they'll hurt us?"

Tii-Eldii didn't answer. He grabbed Jett by the wrist and led him to the rear of the cave. Once inside the deepest cavern, Tii-Eldii pushed a large boulder in front of the doorway.

"I highly doubt that'll keep the Aaptuuans out if that's what you're thinking," Jett said sarcastically.

Tii-Eldii turned away from the door. In the wall, behind where the boulder had been was a large round tunnel. It was easily three meters across. Jett approached it and looked inside. The tunnel disappeared into the darkness. Jett felt its walls. They were completely smooth, like polished glass.

"Is that where we're going?" Jett asked.

Tii-Eldii moved Jett away from the tunnel, stepped into it, and bowed his head. He emitted a deep low hum. The hum echoed into the dark tunnel amplifying itself as it went. Tii-Eldii layered notes, one over the other in a soulful melody.

The chords petered out into silence. Tii-Eldii stood motionless for a few moments. Then, very softly at first, Jett heard the chords repeating themselves in reverse. The melody grew louder as it approached and entered the chamber with a deafening whoosh.

Before Jett could murmur a word, the ground beneath them began to tremble. Something large was moving in the tunnel, something very, very large. The chorus of a thousand tiny feet raced toward them. The steps slowed down and then they ceased altogether. Jett bent forward curiously.

Tii-Eldii stepped back from the tunnel. He held a pumpkin sized red gourd in one of his tentacles. He held the gourd out and made a clicking sound with his claw on the tunnel wall. A large earthworm head emerged, its mouth wide open. Tii-Eldii placed the red gourd inside. As the giant worm crunched down on it, Tii-Eldii placed his claw on the worm's enormous head, and motioned for Jett to come over to him.

"You want me to stand next to that thing?"

Tii-Eldii motioned to Jett more urgently.

"You're not going to feed me to it are you?"

Tii-Eldii turned back to the worm and gently stroked its head. He removed his claw from the creature and placed it on Jett's forehead.

"Jett, this creature is a Lanedaarian pocket worm. It is

going to take us away from here. It will take us to my ship."

"What kind of ship? A boat or raft or something?"

"No, Jett. This worm will take us to my space ship hidden deep inside the planet. The Aaptuuans have yet to find it and they scan this system every ten seasonal cycles."

"How do you know?"

"I listen to their transmissions. We are going to my ship so we can listen for them."

"And exactly how is this frighteningly big worm going to get us there? I can't see any way to ride it. Is it going to eat us and crap us out on the other side?"

"No, Jett, why would you think such a thing? The Lanedaarian pocket worm has large pockets on each of its lateral sides. These are generally used to carry as many as three hundred young, but today, they will carry us and our things. We will ride inside the pockets. Come let me show you."

"That sounds disgusting. I think I'd rather be captured by the Aaptuuans," Jett quipped.

Grabbing Jett forcefully by his wrist, Tii-Eldii pulled him over to the pocket worm. "Stand here," he ordered.

Jett did as he was told. Tii-Eldii removed his claw and began clicking it again. The pocket worm came out of the tunnel and slid past Tii-Eldii. He approached it. It opened its mouth and Tii-Eldii placed another red gourd inside.

"I really want to know where you're hiding those things," Jett said in amazement.

Tii-Eldii walked over to the worm's side. He pulled open a large slimy flap.

"And you expect me to get in there. That's disgusting! Not happening..."

Tii-Eldii picked Jett up and carried him over to the pocket. "It is best not to think about it," he said.

Jett winced and tried to struggle free, "Put me down. Seriously! That's nasty." But Tii-Eldii didn't listen to Jett. Instead he stuffed him into the slimy pocket head first. Jett tried his best to get comfortable, but it was truly a futile exercise unless one enjoyed cold sliminess. He felt a few final tugs on the worm and then everything was still.

A slimy tentacle wrapped itself around Jett's wrist and he screamed, "Get me out of here. This isn't funny."

Tii-Eldii's claw returned to his forehead. "It's alright, Jett," Tii-Eldii comforted. "Get cozy. The journey before us will take some time. Let me tell you my story..."

Chapter 14
Dance of the Pocket Worms

"Entering the Lanedaarian system. Quantum disturbances detected on Lanedaar 3. I think we have found Jett," Chi-Col said as he adjusted the speed and trajectory of the Aaptuuan craft.

"I have confirmed that the Quantum disturbances are consistent with those caused by Jett's exchanger. If he is here then he is trapped. He only had enough power to make two jumps," Le-Wa responded. "Activating Jett's tracking chip."

Le-Wa stood at his console and awaited confirmation from the tracker, but there was no response. "Amplifying signal," he said. He waited a few moments, but there was still no reply.

"It is probable that the chip was temporarily disabled or rendered nonfunctional by the exchange," offered Chi-Col.

"That is likely the case," Le-Wa agreed, "but we will need to conduct a biometric scan of the planet to be certain. As there are no other Solarian life forms, we should locate Jett quickly provided he has survived the surface's harsh conditions."

The Aaptuuan craft passed Lanedaar's lone moon and swooped in on the day-lit side of the planet.

"Setting course for the location of the last quantum disturbance."

"Commencing biometric scan of the area," Le-Wa confirmed.

"Quantum disturbances have occurred within the last 60 cycles. The atomic structure of the surrounding matter is still in secondary reconfiguration phase. Bringing up the location."

The rocky red sand and boulders of Lanedaar's vast deserts appeared before them. The image came into finer relief as they zoomed in on the spot where Jett had materialized just a few short Lanedaarian days earlier.

"Look here," Le-Wa called out, "Solarian footprints leading off into the desert."

Chi-Col turned away from his controls and looked up at the image. They observed footprints magically appearing in the middle of a vast wasteland and leading off in the direction of the foothills in the distance. The unmistakable sneaker tread confirmed that Jett was indeed wandering the surface of Lanedaar 3. Chi-Col brought the craft down to within five meters of the footprints.

Le-Wa frantically interacted with multiple holographic controls, "Biometric residue confirms the tracks belong to Jett. He arrived 6.3 cycles ago."

The tracks on the screen flashed orange and red as they receded toward the horizon.

"Jett was followed," Le-Wa continued as dozens of light blue lines appeared around Jett's footprints, "By charlatones. A great number of them followed him as he made his way toward the bluffs."

They followed Jett's flashing sneaker prints and the bluish highlighted charlatone lines for a few hundred meters. The red tracks stopped, doubled back a few meters, and were encircled by myriad blue lines.

"Here is something strange," Le-Wa observed. "These tracks here," he said pointing at the screen, "these don't resemble anything native to Lanedaar 3 or the Lanedaarian system. This is a creature from another system altogether. Biometric trace readings indicate that the creature who made these tracks is from the Fabboett system: Fabboan Suprema."

"Fabboan Suprema?" Chi-Col asked surprised. "The Fabboett system was neutralized nearly 388,922 cycles ago..."

"These are the tracks of a refugee. A discovery such as this is not without precedent. From time to time there are members of neutralized species who manage to escape the final sweep. This appears to be one of those cases. We must find them both. This Fabboan may have intervened and saved Jett. Either way, Jett's tracks end here, and the Fabboan's tracks lead to that rock formation."

The Aaptuuans followed the tracks at slightly higher altitude so as to avoid detection. The tracks ended, but biometric traces led up to a large red boulder at the base of a tall bluff.

"This area is rich with Fabboan readings. A scan of the hillside indicates an intricate network of tunnels and caves going very deep into the planet's crust. There does not appear to be any Fabboan or Solarian life forms inside at the moment."

"I am bringing the ship down so that we may conduct a more thorough analysis of this subterranean network," Le-Wa offered.

Their ship silently descended to within a few meters of the red gravel surface and hovered there. A hatch appeared on the underside of the craft and lowered itself to the rocky sand. Le-Wa and Chi-Col emerged. Le-Wa carried a scanner. Chi-Col carried a long thin silver staff. The two approached the boulder as the hatch closed silently behind them.

Chi-Col pointed his staff at the boulder and it rolled away to reveal the entrance to Tii-Eldii's cave.

Chi-Col's staff illuminated the empty cave. Bio-traces left by Tii-Eldii and Jett were everywhere. Even without the Aaptuuans' sophisticated equipment, it would have been very obvious to anyone with a flashlight that the cave had been recently inhabited. The red sandy floor of the cave was awash in footprints including those of Jett's size seven Converse All-Stars.

Chi-Col continued into the next cavern. His staff lit the way before him. It was in the second chamber he noticed the beautiful murals of Lanedaarian landscapes. The empty ledges were covered with dustless polygons marking the places where objects were once displayed.

"Look here," Chi-Col said as he pointed to the paintings and polygons.

"They left in a hurry. They must have anticipated our arrival. The Fabboan will know much of our capabilities and has likely taken Jett deep into the planet to avoid detection. Readings indicate they went in that direction," Le-Wa said as he pointed down one of the long dark tunnels.

They followed the readings like hound dogs tracking a fox. They came to a large archway leading to the inner most chamber. It was blocked from inside by a large boulder. Chi-Col's staff burned a bright blue-white and the boulder rolled to one side. They entered the room together.

"Strangely, the readings end in this room," Le-Wa observed, "and I'm detecting a large tunnel entrance just behind the boulder we moved to gain entry. The tunnel is of a size and shape consistent with that of a mature Lanedaarian pocket worm. It appears they have used it to escape. We will need to return to our ship in order to conduct a deep scan of the planet's crust."

But before the Aaptuuans left the chamber, they placed a tiny sensor on its far wall and carefully moved the boulder to precisely the spot it was in before they arrived. They meticulously erased all signs of their visit as they made their way back to entrance. Finally, they replaced the outside boulder and boarded their ship.

"Taking us up to optimal scanning range," Chi-Col said, "that Fabboan may have saved Jett from the charlatones, but he has made our job significantly more time consuming."

"It is reasonable to believe that the Fabboan would see us as a threat, but Solaris 3 need not suffer the same fate as Fabboett."

"If we are unable to locate Jett in time, Solaris 3 will be neutralized."

"An unfortunate reality for his species."

"Commencing biometric scan of the Lanedaarian crust," Chi-Col announced.

On the monitors in front of them, millions of pocket worms coursed through the planet's tunnels in every direction in a hypnotic pulsating dance.

"Now we must be patient and wait."

Chapter 15
Tii-Eldii's Tale

The pocket worm's pouch was a bit tighter and slimier than Jett preferred as far as travel accommodations were concerned. The Aaptuuans had at least figured out a slime free way to travel cocoon style. Being inside a pocket worm was far more unpleasant. Worse still, he didn't expect to find a hot shower and clean clothes waiting for him on the other side.

"Jett, we have some time before us. I would like to tell you of how I came to be on this planet and what I believe became of my civilization."

"Exactly how much time do we have left in here?" Jett asked as he squirmed around uneasily.

"Exactly enough time for me to tell you my tale. No more, no less."

"Well, if it will get my mind off of being stuck in this slime hole..." Jett trailed off.

"I suppose this method of transportation is strange to you. It was for me at first, too, but I soon discovered it was the safest and most efficient mode of transportation available to me. I have never had a gull snake happen upon me when traveling in this fashion."

"I think I'd prefer the gull snake!" challenged Jett.

"You would be surprised what one can get used to," Tii-Eldii replied. "Mine was a very advanced race of space mariners. The idea of traveling in this fashion would have been very foreign to even the basest of my brethren."

"Where are you from?"

"I am not sure the name of my planet would mean

anything to you, but I am from Boona. It is the fourth planet in a system containing eight habitable planets out of the nineteen circling our sun. The planet we are on at this moment is located some twenty-three years travel from my home."

"You mean you sat on a ship by yourself for twenty-three years? That must've been boring as hell."

"If it *seemed* like twenty-three years, you would be right, but at near light speed, time has little meaning and passes very quickly. So I arrived here in what appeared to me to be a time frame similar to our journey today."

"So it felt like it took forever," Jett said sarcastically.

"No, it did not, it felt like..."

"I get it. I get it," interrupted Jett, "you obviously don't have sarcasm where you're from. Anyway, please continue."

"As I was saying, my home is twenty-three light years from here and I arrived on this planet sixty-five of its years ago. On my world, I was a preeminent astrophysicist studying advanced propulsion technologies. My people had been traveling between our eight habitable planets and various colonies and space stations for many centuries, but space transport was a slow and a cumbersome process and it took months to travel between the most distant settlements. My government commissioned me and my friend, Ripeem, to lead a team of scientists whose task it was to find a faster way to transport both Boonans and goods in our solar system and beyond.

"We knew if we found a faster way to travel, we would also need to develop a faster way to communicate. After several months of experimentation, my team stumbled upon a new subspace frequency that would allow for nearly instantaneous communication between all corners of our system and beyond. This discovery was revolutionary and would allow for our civilization's expansion to remote systems.

"Almost immediately we began intercepting strange transmissions. We recorded them, analyzed them, and tried to decipher them, but to no avail. I issued strict orders, under penalty of death, that no one was to outfit the communications platform with a transmitter. We were to remain in listen only mode until we could decode the strange language and assess if the voices were those of friend or foe.

"You see, we had been a space faring species for generations, and had already encountered life on other planets, but we were always the most technologically advanced and were able to enslave or exterminate troublesome species with relative ease. We brought the entire solar system under our control in a matter of a few generations, and we dedicated a museum to the species we wiped out.

"Still for all this discovery and conquest, we had never encountered another space faring species. While the idea of other more advanced civilizations existing out there among the billions of galaxies was generally accepted, the lack of contact with any such beings gave my race a certain hubris as we spread throughout our system.

"As you might imagine, the denizens of those planets we colonized didn't always surrender easily. The most determined were exterminated, wiped from the galactic records," Tii-Eldii paused for a moment before continuing, "It was for these crimes, The Fold, as we would come to know them later, held us to account." Tii-Eldii paused again. Jett could feel him release a deep sigh-like breath.

"While we were hopping from planet to planet building our empire, they watched, catalogued, and recorded our brutality. It was not enough that acts of violence between members of our own species, most especially murder, were exceedingly rare, except in cases of treason; that we killed other species for any reason at all was enough to violate the first tenant of The Ten Laws: Do not kill others.

"The religious among us touted the Ten Laws of Civilized Living most especially: Never murder a fellow Boonan. It turns out we had a slight misunderstanding of that particular law. Membership into The Fold means that you will not kill any sentient being for any reason including hunger."

"You mean they want us to all be vegetarians?" interrupted Jett.

"Yes, The Fold requires their members to have a diet derived from non-sentient sources. This often, but not always, includes plant based life forms."

"How do you know so much about The Fold?"

"Well," continued Tii-Eldii, "It was those radio transmissions I started describing to you. The transmissions we intercepted were those of The Fold and the Aaptuuan deep space missions. I was working late one night alone in the laboratory, running the recorded transmissions through another decryption algorithm when suddenly the voices became clear. At first I didn't understand what they were saying, I could only make out the inflections, but we Boonans have a knack for language as I'm certain you've noticed. Within a few hours I could make out words and simple phrases. Within a couple weeks, I could understand the transmissions almost entirely.

"For security reasons, I kept this information strictly to myself. I was afraid that the government and military might overreact if they overheard select snippets referring to a 'Neutralization' protocol. I wanted to understand what The Fold meant by neutralization and if we were the target. I had no real way of knowing who was generating these transmissions, who was receiving them, or to whom or what they were in reference to.

"I did know a couple of things. I knew there was a race that was potentially far more advanced than ours. I knew that they were monitoring hundreds and possibly thousands of civilizations, and I knew that they were actively determining the fates of those civilizations in real time.

"Due to the nature of the transmissions, I kept the decryption algorithm a secret. For the next several months I listened to them in my study late into the night. My wife, Ekiwoo, became increasingly concerned as my lack of sleep was expressing itself in both my haggard appearance and unsavory disposition.

"There was one thing that bothered me above all else. I couldn't determine whether or not these beings were monitoring our system. I never heard anything that sounded like Boona or like any of the other planetary names I was familiar with.

"Late one night I fell asleep in my study while reviewing the day's recordings. I found myself on a small ship with two diminutive white creatures who were staring at an image of Boona on a screen from the ship's bridge. I heard them repeat the same words over and over.

'Fabboett Four, Fabboett Four, Fabboett Four...'

"I awoke with a start. Fabboett, I'd heard this name referred to many times along with thousands of others, but Fabboett had an eerie frequency to it. I decided that the only way I could prove Fabboett referred to Boona was to calculate the strength of the transmissions themselves.

"I immediately interfaced with my computer and found a strong correlation between the frequency of the word Fabboett and the strength of the transmission. Then I did something I hadn't done in a few days. Rather than review recorded transmissions, I switched to a slightly delayed live feed and selected for transmissions containing the word Fabboett. What I found was that transmissions containing the word Fabboett had either very high or extremely low field strength. Selecting for the high field strength, I determined that half of these transmissions were originating from *within* our solar system.

"The discovery caught me by surprise. It now appeared that there was an advanced species monitoring us from within our own solar system and we were completely unaware of it. Somehow, even after we had charted and mapped every corner of our solar system, this race had managed to evade our detection. This revelation was quite alarming.

"I had to tell someone I trusted, so I told my wife.

'Are you sure,' Ekiwoo asked me? 'You do not want a thing such as this to leak out. It would cause a panic.'

"I assured her that we were the only ones who knew and that I had not planned on sharing the news with anyone else just yet. I needed to assess the progress of the advanced propulsion project. I hadn't checked in on it since we intercepted those first alien transmissions.

"To my surprise, during my absence a breakthrough had occurred which would allow our space mariners to travel near the speed of light. While still hypothetical, the team had already gone to work on a light speed vehicle. Primary to their mission was the development of a super strong material that could withstand the impact of space debris at incredible speeds.

"My friend, Ripeem, had discovered a way to isolate and store Ionecs. These particles travel at the speed of light and if stored and directed can propel a craft nearly as fast. Dr. Ripeem was in the process of testing our first light speed vehicle, a small ball the sized of Nukii, when I arrived at the lab.

'Tii-Eldii, we've missed you here at the propulsion lab,' he said, "Have you been well?"

'I'm sure you've heard of my discovery,' I replied.

'Discovery?' Ripeem asked.

"I pulled Ripeem to the side, away from the others, and told him of the signals we'd intercepted.

'I've heard the rumors,' he said, 'and I chalked them up to sub-space noise.'

'It is not noise,' I told him, 'They're watching us.'

'Who's watching us?'

'The Aaptuuans. The Fold. At this very moment, they are contemplating the fate of our solar system, our species,' I said. 'We are so very close to being neutralized.'

'Neutralized? The Fold? You are not making sense.'

'The Fold, whatever that is, determines the fate of all advanced species in the galaxy. They are monitoring us from *inside our own solar system*,' I emphasized, "I decoded some of their transmissions.'

'That's impossible. We've explored every square inch of this system. If there was another advanced race here, we would know about it.'

'Would we? What if they are not of this solar system?'

"Ripeem paused and thought about it for a moment, 'Who have you told?'

'You and Ekiwoo,' I answered.

'When are you planning to tell the Elders?'

'After I discussed it with you. I wanted you to review the transmissions for accuracy. There's no need to alarm the populace if it is only electromagnetic interference.'

'Ok,' he said, 'Right after we complete this test.'

"Ripeem led me back to the control console. On the wall were two large monitors. The one on the left displayed a satellite which held a Nukii sized silver ball. The monitor on the right displayed a satellite with a Nukii sized receiver.

"The first was positioned in space between Boona and our second moon. The second satellite was positioned in an orbit around Bionaw, our solar system's fourteenth planet. It would normally take thirty-three units to travel from Boona to Bionaw. The goal was to see how much faster Dr. Ripeem's propulsion system would make the trip.

"The central government declared the ball's anticipated path a no fly zone. Success in this endeavor would open a whole new frontier of space exploration and colonization. It would mean vast new resources and riches."

Tii-Eldii paused again.

"And..." Jett coaxed.

"And fame and fortune for my friend Ripeem and me,"

Tii-Eldii lamented, "and where was I, oh yes, the experiment...
'Confirm launch trajectory,' Ripeem ordered.

'Confirmed,' a technician responded.

'Commence launch sequence. 5, 4, 3, 2, 1...'

"The silver ball disappeared from the right monitor appearing to go in multiple directions at once before disappearing entirely into nothingness. Everyone in the room stared in anticipation at the receiver satellite on the left. A counter ticked the elapsing time until after 2.3999 units the silver ball appeared on the other side. The room erupted cheerfully. The silver ball was mutilated almost beyond recognition.

'Space debris,' Ripeem said, 'can be quite brutal at these speeds. Protecting against it is our next challenge. It's time to celebrate,' he said, 'You should join us.'

'How can I refuse?' I replied. This was a gigantic leap forward for our people and we'd both be rich beyond measure. His propulsion. My radio. There was nothing to stop us, nothing, that is, except for these confounded transmissions.

"That night we relished in possibility and fantasized about how we'd spend our fortunes.

'I am going to buy my own asteroid,' Ripeem declared after several drinks. 'I'm going to name it Kewo after my eldest offspring. I know just the place in the sun-belt between Ahle and Kyskerlaw. What are you going to do with yours?' he asked me.

'I'm going to pay off each of my offspring's pods and maybe buy a little summer place on the coast,' I reply modestly.

'Oh, you lack imagination,' Ripeem teased. 'You'll be

able to do a lot more than that! Another drink for my unimaginative friend.'

"As the evening wore on I'm suddenly taken by the thought that Ripeem's experiment today might have caught the attention of The Fold. This is just the sort of thing they'd be looking for.

'I'm going to the restroom,' I lied knowing full well that Ripeem would never let me take off so early.

"After leaving the cantina, I went directly home and reviewed the recordings leading up to and immediately following the test. The intercepts confirmed my worst fears.

'Fabboett lightspeed test completed. Threat assessment underway.'

'Neutralization protocol activated. Deploying resources to Fabboett system.'

'Activating Fabboett asteroid relay network.'

'Preparing Fabboett neutralization simulations.'

'Confirmed Fabboett neutralization links active.'

'Fabboett threat assessment completed. Maintain high alert.'

"All I could think was, 'Oh, Thoh! How could it come to this?' We were perched on the brink of annihilation or whatever came after a neutralization had run its course. It was the end of times. The end of everything."

Chapter 16
The End of Times

"I witnessed it," Jett said softly.

"Witnessed what?" Tii-Eldii asked.

"A neutralization. Before I came here I watched the Aaptuuans neutralize a system. It was terrifying. I don't want them to do it to Earth."

"Like you, I alone knew The Fold was weighing the fate of my people. It is a heavy burden you bear."

"How did you deal with it? Did you warn them?"

"As I was saying, it was quite a shock to hear the Aaptuuans roll out the neutralization protocol so precisely and moreover, so flatly. I was paralyzed as I listened to the transmissions.

'Fabboett neutralization relay network simulation testing complete. Relay network fully operational.'

'Outer sweep of Fabboett system commencing. Deep space asset identification and inventory underway.'

'Fabboett threat level remains high. Maintain assessment phase.'

I thought about these voices and why, if they were so advanced, would they react in this manner to a single light speed test? How would they react if they knew I was listening? How could I tell my people without invoking panic or being labeled a lunatic?

I tried reaching Ripeem on his radio link, but he did not pick up. My multiple calls went unanswered. Ripeem and his team would need to cease all light speed testing.

I decided if I could not reach him, I would leave for his

106

laboratory straight away and wait for him there. Walking through the streets, I marveled at the tall elegant skyscrapers and the millions of twinkling lights shining in the windows. I closed my eyes and imagined all of my fellow citizens as they watched the night's news or highlights from the day's games. I imagined them putting their offspring to bed or enjoying a late night snack in blissful ignorance of the events that were about to unfold.

It was hard for me to imagine a society as advanced as Boona suddenly 'switched off' by some mysterious extraterrestrial race for reasons yet unknown. After all, we weren't an especially violent species as species go.

As I mentioned before, murder of Boonans by Boonans was practically nonexistent, and with the exception of very remote settlements, subjugation of less advanced societies was no longer necessary. Life was peaceful and abundant for someone of my stature and was about to become even more so. Oh, to think of the riches even now..." Tii-Eldii trailed off.

"Maybe that's why they did it," Jett commented after a while.

"What are you referring to?"

"The riches. The conquest."

"Perhaps," Tii-Eldii replied, "I am sure both were factors. We were far from perfect in regards to many of The Ten Laws."

"So why do you think they did it?"

"I have had much time to reflect on that question. I believe it was the way in which we integrated other societies into our own. The first colonizations were a bloody affair, but over time we learned to take a gentler approach. At the time of

107

the neutralization, subjugated species were the cogs that powered our civilization. They grew our food. They cleaned our homes. They made great pets. They prospered."

"So then what happened?"

"I raced to Ripeem's lab, but it was empty. They were all still out celebrating. I sat down at one of the work terminals and fell asleep. That night I dreamed of the settlements of Boona belching fire and I suffered the screams of the dying.

Then I was jolted awake.

"Good morning sleepy head. Couldn't wait to get back to work?" Ripeem teased.

"Ripeem, you have to stop the tests!"

"What are you talking about? You obviously drank too much slog last night."

"You don't understand, they are about to neutralize our solar system."

"Who is?"

"The Fold."

"The Fold is going to neutralize our solar system? You sound insane. You'd better pull it together or you could blow this for both of us. We're on the cusp of something big here. Revolutionary."

"I understand that, but you need to come with me, and listen for yourself."

After some coaxing, Ripeem finally agreed to join me for 'a quick listen' and soon the seriousness of the situation was evident to him.

"They mean to shut down everything, absolutely everything? Why?"

"From what I know, they feel your light speed

propulsion system poses a significant threat to galactic peace."

"Do they suppose we're going to burn and pillage our way across the galaxy?"

"Well, that is exactly what we did in our own system. Even now, those we conquered centuries ago remain our servants and pets. Abuses persist in the remote colonies."

"We are far from perfect, granted, but we are not mindless killers. What right do they have to enforce their will on us?"

"Unless we figure out a way to stop them, they don't need a right."

Ripeem and I sat for the next several hours and listened to the recordings. We evaluated strategies we would use to share this sensitive information with The Elders, knowing full well we might be labeled 'unfit for service'.

In the end, we decided to risk our reputations and inform The Elders. We hurried to their chambers and requested an immediate audience.

Much to our surprise, our request was granted. We entered the opulent chamber. The Elders sat in plush blue chairs around a large round table. The room itself was comprised of glass walls that offered enviable views of the city.

"What urgent business brings you here?" Thardulma, head of the Council of Elders, demanded.

"The information we share here today is for The Elders' ears alone. Discretion is of the utmost importance," I began.

"Very well," Thardulma granted. "Leave us," he commanded with a wave. Servants, aids, and staff filed out of the chamber. The doors closed behind them with a succession of heavy thuds.

When they had all gone, Thardulma said, "Please proceed."

I shared my discovery of the alien signals and their chilling message. I told them that whoever The Fold was had no idea I was listening to them. Then I played several of the translated recordings to The Council and explained the need to immediately cease all light speed testing.

"Leave us," Thardulma said, "We require time to discuss what you have told us."

"Yes, Thardulma," we replied in unison and showed ourselves out.

Ripeem and I waited outside for a very long time. Eventually, the chamber doors opened and Thardulma motioned to us to come in.

"Please, my friends, have a seat," he said motioning to two chairs at the opposite end of the table. "The news you bring us is quite troubling. You must tell us who knows of the recordings."

"Just us in this chamber," I answered.

"You mentioned your staff knows of the radio."

"They know of the transmissions only as noise, and are unaware I've decrypted and translated them."

"No outgoing transmissions have been made?" Thardulma pressed.

"No. None. They are unaware we are listening," I continued. "I believe that as long as we don't test the light speed propulsion system again, we can avert this crisis."

"How can you be sure?"

"I can't, Thardulma," I replied.

"Unfortunately, The Council of Elders is of the same

opinion. We must prepare for the worst."

"Will we alert the citizenry?" Ripeem asked.

"No, we cannot. To do so would cause panic."

"What will we do then?" I asked.

"We will build twelve arks. They will carry key citizens, supplies, our libraries - the knowledge of 25,000 years far away from here. They will be outfitted with your new propulsion and communications systems. We will gather vessels we deem most suited for the mission in the Capitol Hanger along with our best engineers, technicians, materials scientists, astrophysicists, and librarians. This project is highly classified. You will tell no one."

"Of course, Thardulma," we said in unison.

"Not your life partners, not your offspring, no one."

"Yes, no one," Ripeem and I answered.

"Good. Meet us in the Capital Hanger at first light tomorrow morning."

We nodded in agreement and were dismissed. I was ordered to go home, gather up all of the recordings and other data I had collected and bring it with me to the hanger. As we exited the building, I took in a bustling city precariously perched on a razor's edge. I wanted to scream, "Run for your lives. Gather supplies, go home, and hunker down! It's the end of the world!" but to do so would only serve to get me locked up. No sense in experiencing the end of the world from a prison cell.

"Heavy duty," Ripeem whispered to me as we made our way through the crowded street. "You OK?"

"I do not think now is the time or place to discuss this."

"I'm just asking if you're ok."

I shook my head, no, bid him farewell and pressed on through the streets.

"I'll see you at zero dark hundred," I heard Ripeem say before he was swallowed by the evening crowd.

Back at my lab, I went about my tasks in a foggy haze. Concerned colleagues, interns, and servants inquired about my wellbeing, but I dismissed them with uninspired stories of revelry from my night with Ripeem, whose reputation as both a brilliant scientist and party animal were well known. Afterward, I went home. My wife, Ekiwoo, seemed very concerned by my frazzled state and insisted I go straight to bed. She made me a warm cup of larva juice.

"I do not approve of your gallivanting around town with Ripeem. One of these days he's going to get you in a heap of trouble!"

"Like today?" I wearily asked.

"Precisely. Look at yourself, you're a shadow."

She was right. I was a shadow. Shock and disbelief wracked my mind. What had I done? I could hardly hold it together. Despair was written all over my face. I had to pull it together. Boona was counting on me. So I took a deep breath, looked up at Ekiwoo and said, "You are right. I need to get some sleep. We can talk about it in the morning. Good night."

Ekiwoo must have put a sedative in my larva juice, because I finally woke up to my comm-link buzzing frantically on the table next to my head. I answered it, "Hello?"

"Where are you?" Ripeem demanded, "The Elders are very concerned you're not here yet."

I sat up in bed and realized that I had overslept - by a lot.

"I will be there soon," I replied groggily. "Is my team ready?"

"Everyone is here, and we are _all_ waiting for you!"

"Ok, ok," I shouted as I sprung out of bed still wearing the same clothes I'd worn the previous day. I raced into my office, grabbed my recordings, and rushed to The Hanger.

"Nice of you to show up," Thardulma said with a deep seriousness as I sprinted into the hanger.

"Will not happen again, Thardulma."

"I expect it won't." Thardulma addressed those gathered before him. "These are dark times," he began, "Tii-Eldii and his team have discovered hostile alien transmissions originating in our own solar system. These presumably more advanced extraterrestrials are at this very moment monitoring our activities and deciding our fate.

"Our military is on high alert. They are searching our solar system for signs of these creatures and their neutralization devices, but so far none have been found. The only evidence we have of their existence are the translated recordings Tii-Eldii has provided. These have been given to a team of linguistics experts for confirmation. Ripeem, you are to retrofit these crafts with your propulsion and advanced shielding systems." Then he turned to me. "You Tii-Eldii will act as a distraction."

"I am not sure I understand what you mean, Thardulma."

"After you have installed your radio system on these crafts, you will use it to cause a distraction. We have sent your designs to outposts throughout the system. They are building transmitters."

113

"Are you sure that's a good idea? What if they alert the aliens to our eavesdropping?"

"You will disrupt The Fold's communications long enough for the arks to get away. You will surge their own signals."

"Then what?"

"We pray."

Our secret work progressed in earnest. Within a few short months the twelve arks were surreptitiously outfitted and moved to launch position. They were strategically positioned in twelve specially selected spots in space above Boona. Since they appeared outwardly to be 'normal' Boonan craft, they escaped the attention of The Fold's ever watchful eyes.

Ripeem and I were paired up to pilot one of the vessels. All were scheduled to launch the following morning. I left the Capitol Hanger early and went home to spend what would be my last evening with Ekiwoo. We talked of our life together and of our offspring, and our grand-kin. We reminisced late into the night.

After Ekiwoo fell asleep, I slipped a time delayed message into her comm-link and left for the hanger. I knew I wouldn't be able to sleep that night. Every moment I spent with Ekiwoo hurt me deeply because I knew that I'd probably never see her again. To prepare her for whatever was to come, I amassed food and supplies and prayed to Thoh to take care of my family in my absence.

That night I slept in the chair of my temporary office at the Capitol Hanger. Ripeem shook me awake.

"Got here early, huh." He said.

"Yes," I replied flatly.

"Time to go."

We dressed for our mission and went to the shuttle that would take us to our ark. I stared out the window at the world we built over millennia and marveled at its sudden and utter fragility.

As we prepared to launch Ripeem asked, "Do you think we'll ever see it again?"

"No."

"I'm afraid I have to agree," he replied glumly.

"Here goes nothing," I said as I activated the transmission jammer.

As anticipated, the blast blinded The Fold to our activities and we managed to launch all twelve arks. Luckily, most of the arks made it out of our solar system undetected. Mine was among these.

"We have to slow down," Ripeem warned, "The stress on the vehicle is too great."

"What if they catch us?"

"If they were going to catch us, they would have done it by now. If we don't slow down, the ship will break apart and all this would've been for nothing."

Reluctantly I gave in. I looked down at the elapsed time and realized that what seemed like a few minutes to Ripeem and me marked the passage of several weeks. I stared at the date and time in disbelief.

"There must be something wrong with the clocks," I observed.

"No they are fine, at this speed, the fabric of time itself has warped. We have been traveling for over three weeks in relation to the time we understand."

I turned on the radio and listened to it furiously as I tried to determine the fate of Boona.

"Fabboett neutralization complete," is what I hear.

"It is over," I say glumly, "They have destroyed everything."

Our craft was violently jolted.

"What was that?" I ask.

"Space debris. It appears to have penetrated our shielding and hit one of our stabilizers. I'll need to go outside to fix it."

"It is too dangerous. You must stay inside with me."

"It's far more dangerous if I stay inside. If we don't repair the stabilizer, the rest of the propulsion system is at risk. You don't want to drift aimlessly in space for all eternity, do you?"

Actually, at this point, I am not sure I would have minded such a fate since there was nothing left for me on Boona, but instead I said, "You are right."

"Good then, we agree," Ripeem replied with a smile as he put on his space suit and headed into the airlock. "See you in a few minutes."

Ripeem stepped outside into the blackness of space and gently guided himself along the top of our vessel until he had reached the stabilizer housing.

"It's an easy fix. I'll be done in a snap."

"A snap," I thought, "As if a snap meant anything anymore after I witnessed weeks pass in a matter of minutes."

"All finished," Ripeem reported over the intercom, "I'm going to give the rest of the propulsion system a quick once over while I'm out here."

Ripeem guided himself to the rear of the craft to begin his inspection. A second piece of debris slammed into the ship. It dislodged Ripeem and sent him spinning off into space.

"Ripeem!" I screamed, but there was no reply, "Ripeem!"

A third rock smashed the ship, then a fourth, and finally a full on volley of meteorites pummeled the craft. Ripeem's biometric readings flat lined. He was dead. The impact had killed him. I attempted to turn the ship around to retrieve Ripeem, but his body disappeared into a nebulous cloud of dust and rocks. His tracking chip went dead. Ripeem was lost and if I did not get the ark out of there fast, I would be, too.

Debris continued to slam into the ark as I piloted it through an endless sea of meteorites. I eventually cleared the debris field and corrected my course for Lanedaar 3 - a planet I had learned of through my Aaptuuan radio intercepts.

I now had decades of solitude before me to consider the fate of my people, my family, and my friend, Ripeem. It was the end of times. I would complete my mission, arrive on Lanedaar, and wait for a sign from The Elders.

Here I am all these long years later, still waiting, and now you are here..."

Chapter 17
In the Nick of Time Warp

Jett felt the giant worm's body come to a slow rolling stop.

"We've arrived," Tii-Eldii said.

"Great! Can I get out of here now?"

Tii-Eldii, covered in slime from head to toe, climbed out of the worm first. Then he reached back in with several slimy tentacles and extracted Jett from the worm's pouch and set him down on the floor of a large dimly lit cave. Ooze dripped from his body. Perched in its center was an alien spacecraft. Nukii shot out of Tii-Eldii's pocket, landed on the ground, and shook herself off like a small dog. Sepia color slime sprayed everywhere.

Jett remarked, "You suppose next time maybe we could take your spaceship?"

"If we took my spaceship, the Aaptuuans would detect us. This cavern sits beneath hundreds of kilometers of active worm tunnels crisscrossing thousands of kilometers of highly magnetic iron ore deposits. Together, they act as a natural shield from the Aaptuuan scans."

Jett looked up. He realized that he understood Tii-Eldii perfectly without any sort of physical contact. "Wait," he said, "How did you do that?"

"How did I do what?" Tii-Eldii asked.

"And you aren't touching me, but I can understand what you're saying."

"Earlier than I expected and likely due to our prolonged contact in the pocket worm."

"You knew this would happen?"

"Of course. My species developed the ability to communicate with others in this manner before we set out on our first space missions. For a hundred generations, physical contact was required. Then a litter of young ones changed that forever. They could communicate without physical contact after prolonged exposure to another Boonan.

"Within a couple generations descendants of this litter could communicate with domesticated species, and now apparently with you. We can't read thoughts. We only transmit them, so your secrets are safe," he chuckled, "Not all of my brethren can communicate in this way, but I am a descendant of that special litter."

"Well, good. I was getting tired of you touching me all the time anyway," Jett said as he attempted to wipe the goo off himself.

Tii-Eldii made a noise that might have been a laugh and opened his beak wide. Out snaked a long tongue more than two meters long. A suction cup sat delicately on its tip. Tii-Eldii then proceeded to vacuum himself off with his tongue. Worse, he appeared to enjoy it — a little too much.

"Would you like me to clean you off, too?"

"You're kidding me right? I'm, ah, gonna head over to the spaceship and see if you have any towels or tablecloths or sheets I can wipe myself off with."

Jett waddled awkwardly toward the ship, clumps of slime splattering to the ground around him. Nukii followed closely. The slime was now cold and uncomfortable against his skin. The cool dankness of the cave wasn't helping matters much. The slime in his shoes slushed as he walked.

119

Tii-Eldii's tongue retracted back into his mouth in a flash. "Jett wait!" he cried.

Suddenly a large rock rose up on six long legs and pivoted around. It had the look of an Alaskan king crab, but stood nearly three meters tall and had two enormous fang lined mouths stacked one above the other. The monster's shell was burgundy red with thin yellow stripes organized in a V-shaped pattern across its underbelly. The monster shimmied toward Jett. Jett, paralyzed by fear was glued to the ground.

"Um, ah, Tii-Eldii...!" Jett wheezed. Drool, now dripping from each of the creature's two mouths, collected in large puddles.

Before he could utter another sound, Jett was lifted off the ground by its giant claw. His feet dangled a meter off the cavern floor. The monster held him so tightly he could hardly breathe.

"Craabic, put it down this instant. Bad boy that's not your supper!" Tii-Eldii ordered waving his tentacles wildly above his head.

The creature sighed and dropped Jett to the ground with a dull thud. Jett gasped for air and quickly scrambled away.

"What is that thing?"

"This is Craabic. He keeps an eye on things down here whenever I'm on the surface, which is most of the time. He's a subterranean rock crab. Craabic, meet Jett."

Jett looked up at Craabic skeptically, "He was going to eat me wasn't he?"

"Definitely. It's a good thing I am here with you. In the wild his species eats pocket worms."

"Why didn't he eat the pocket worm we arrived in?"

"He is not allowed to eat those ones. Besides Craabic prefers dead ones... really dead ones."

"How can he tell the difference?"

"I inject the transport worms with a special scent marker that the subterranean rock crabs find repulsive. Random worms arriving in the cavern generally make an easy meal for Craabic. If he is not hungry, he chases them off so they don't nest in here, ruin my equipment, or generally make a mess of the place."

Jett looked around. As far as caves go, this one was even tidier than the last, and contained even cooler stuff. This place had potential. That spaceship was probably his only hope of restoring his swapper and returning home. As he walked toward the ship, he could see his reflection in its glassy metal shell. He looked absolutely terrible, not that he was shocked. He'd been to hell and back in the last several days. He was covered in slime from head to toe; his hair was slicked up into a tall blue point whose top bent to one side like a sad hook. He smelled like vomit on a hot summer day.

"Seriously, Tii-Eldii, you have to help me here. This is the grossest I've ever looked or stunk in my whole life, and that includes some seriously gory Halloween costumes."

"I actually think you smell a lot better."

"Seriously, is there some place I can wash myself off?"

"Yes, there is water over there."

Jett looked in the direction Tii-Eldii pointed. He squinted hard, but couldn't see more than ten meters into the darkness.

"Where. I can't see anything."

"Let me fix that."

Tii-Eldii turned and activated a panel on the outside of the long cigar shaped craft. The lights popped on and flickered dimly. Jett was astounded by the size of the cavern. It was easily the length of several football fields and had dozens of tunnels leading out in every direction. At the far end of it an underground lake shimmered.

"Before I rush over there like an idiot," Jett asked, "is there anything that might eat me?"

"Probably not," Tii-Eldii replied, "but that was not always the case."

"Great. How are you so sure it's safe now?"

"Because I killed the creature that once occupied the lake soon after I selected this location to house the ark. I did not want to do it, but the creature, a Lanedaarian cave eel, would not leave of its own accord. Nor could it be domesticated like Craabic here. Unfortunately for the cave eel, its cave offered many advantages not readily found elsewhere on the planet."

"How do you know another cave eel or gull snake or worse hasn't taken its place?"

"Craabic sees to it that nothing new moves in. I assure you it is perfectly safe. Take Nukii with you. She loves the water."

Jett wasn't convinced some new threat wasn't waiting for him just beneath the lake's placid surface, but he also couldn't stand another moment of cold, sticky, sliminess.

Nukii raced ahead as he walked to the black pool. It dawned on Jett that if this fuzzy little animal wasn't afraid of the water, neither was he, so he picked up his pace and soon met Nukii at the water's edge.

Jett stopped and looked down into the water's glassy surface. His reflection was one of a hopelessly lost boy, covered in slime, and haggard beyond words. He peeled off his wet clothes and dove into the pool. Its frigid waters shocked the exhaustion out of his body.

"Come on in girl," Jett called, but Nukii happily fiddled at the edge. She collected water in her mouth and sprayed it at Jett. "Hey!" Jett laughed. "If you're going to spray something, spray off my clothes."

Much to Jett's surprise, instead of spraying his clothes, she began eating them.

"Hey, stop that!" Jett demanded.

As he swam over to stop Nukii, Jett felt something brush past his leg.

"Ahhhh!" he screamed, "Tii-Eldii!"

Tii-Eldii turned away from what he was doing and bounded across the cave. Soon he had Jett dangling upside down and, with the exception of his dog tags, stark naked.

"I see you also have a tentacle," Tii-Eldii observed.

"Just put me down," Jett said flatly.

Tii-Eldii did as Jett asked and placed him on the floor next to his clothes. Jett wrestled his clothes away from Nukii, but the damage was done.

"What happened?" Tii-Eldii asked.

"Nukii has eaten holes through all of my clothes!"

"That is what you were screaming about? Your clothing is made out of plant based materials. Of course she ate them. This is hardly a thing to become so excited about."

"No, not the clothes," Jett replied, "there's something

123

else swimming in the water. It brushed past me. I must've scared it off when I screamed."

"Doubtfully. Sulfur eels can't hear or see," Tii-Eldii said as he plucked an iridescent blood red eel out of the water, "but they do make good eating," Tii-Eldii continued as he crunched the eel's ugly eyeless head off in one bite before slipping the rest of its body into his mouth.

"Ok, I didn't need to see that. Do me a favor and don't eat in front of me ever again."

"You don't want to try one?"

"Um, no and certainly not raw, besides I'm vegan," commented Jett as he made his way back to the ark attempting to cover himself with what was left of his ragged clothes.

"Here, you might want to try this on," Tii-Eldii said offering Jett a soft crimson robe he had taken from the Ark.

"Thanks," Jett replied, "my clothes are trashed. I may as well feed the rest to Nukii," he continued tossing his clothes to the ground.

He unwrapped his swapper and fidgeted with it.

"It's completely dead."

"What power source does it use?"

"Some sort of battery pack from Aaptuu 4, but I'm not even sure that's the problem. The machine itself could've been damaged from the two swaps, but without power, I have no way of troubleshooting it."

"I may be able to provide power for your device, Jett, but we need to be very careful. The slightest miscalculation in the amount of power we generate may tip the Aaptuuans off to our location. We're already pushing it with the lights."

"We don't even know if the Aaptuuans are here."

"No we do not, but we can easily find out. Come with me."

Jett followed Tii-Eldii into the ark through an open doorway. Tii-Eldii approached a long control panel and pressed a series of buttons. A low hum emanated from the bowels of the ship. Tii-Eldii turned a knob and Jett heard Aaptuuan voices. They sounded nearly identical to the voices he had heard during his short stay on Aaptuu 4.

"Are those the Aaptuuans?" Jett asked.

"They are predominantly Aaptuuan voices, but there are other voices too; those of other advanced members of The Fold who share the policing burden. However, only the Aaptuuans possess the ability to neutralize systems."

"You can understand what they're saying?"

"Yes. I've been listening to their communications for nearly a century. I am fluent in many of the languages used for these transmissions. Right now the various system sentries are checking in with the Galactic Threat Assessment Center on Aaptuu 5."

They listened to the radio for a long time. Jett couldn't understand a word, so he found a blanket, and curled up in a chair nearby and fell to sleep.

Jett dreamed he was home again. He was in his backyard. There was a BBQ underway, and all of the napkins, cups, and plates were star spangled, red, white, and blue. Classic rock blared in the background. Everyone was there. His mother, father, Jack, Ravi, Stanford, but before Jett could utter a sound, there was a car crash, then a second, and a third followed by a succession of car crashes and explosions.

The music stopped. Ravi stared blankly into his iPhone.

His father and brother rushed out into the street. Jett looked up at the sky and a small single engine plane plummeted toward him. He tried to scream, but nothing came out. Jett sprung awake.

"Ahh, it's started!"

"What's started?" Tii-Eldii asked, "are you OK?"

"The neutralization... The neutralization of Earth."

"You were dreaming. Earth is fine. I've listened to the updates. The Fold is scouring the galaxy to find you. Your invention must be quite something."

"Where are they now?"

"They're here."

"What? The Aaptuuans are here? On Lanedaar 3? When did they get here? Do they know I'm here?"

"Unfortunately, I didn't destroy your tracking chip in time. They received a signal from it and the signal has led them here. They found my cave on the surface. They have searched it, and they now know of me. The good news is they do not know our current location."

"That's a plus. How much time do you think we have?"

"Quite some time if we stay down here and keep the power below detectable levels, but they will not give up easily. They are currently comparing your bio-scan data to that of every creature walking, slithering, or crawling within 100 meters of the surface. Everything will be cataloged and tracked. As soon as you pop up on the surface - they'll have you."

"We need to fix my quantum swapper. If we can fix it, I can get us out of here."

"Where will we go?"

"I can take you home first and then I'll head to Earth. I just need to be sure I'll have enough charge left to make a third swap."

Tii-Eldii thought about it for moment. Home. He never thought he would see it again. "I would very much like that," he said, "How can I help?"

"We need to power it up."

Tii-Eldii led Jett into the rear of the craft. He fetched some strange looking tools, wire, and assorted odds and ends. He rigged power up through a tangle of wires that ran beneath the control console. Jett disassembled the swapper, and organized its various components in front of him.

"We'll need to run power into this port," Jett pointed.

"Got it," Tii-Eldii replied, "first, I will attach this multimeter to determine the device's power requirements."

Tii-Eldii took a series of measurements and said, "This machine of yours requires tremendous power to move objects through space time. The battery pack stores enough energy for exactly two jumps, and it is now depleted."

"Can we recharge it?"

"I am afraid not. This battery is not of a chemistry I'm acquainted with. We will have to power the swapper by wire. That will give us enough for one jump. It will be sufficient to get you home, Jett."

"What about you?"

"I will be on the next worm out of here." Tii-Eldii grinned as he looked over the other components and continued, "In time, my geomagnetic batteries will recharge enough to perform a second swap assuming they don't come down here and neutralize my equipment. Where did you say you got these batteries?"

"The Aaptuuans gave them to me. I was in a room that was my room, only it wasn't. The room talked to me, its name was Bob, and..." Jett told Tii-Eldii how he had acquired everything he needed to build a new swapper which he later used to escape from Tower 100.

"You are telling me the Aaptuuans just gave you everything you needed to escape? I am sorry, Jett, but I find your tale to be illogical. The Aaptuuans can read your thoughts. They knew what you were trying to accomplish. The question is, why?"

"Why, what?"

"Why did they let you escape?"

"No one let me escape!" Jett burst out, "It was the way I asked for the things. I fooled them!"

"You are fooling only yourself. I am sure the Aaptuuans have a plan for you, but your arrival here was not a part of it. They are determined to have you back."

"Well, they're going to have to catch me first! What's it gonna take to fire my swapper up?"

"One gigawatt of power."

"Are you kidding me? The swapper I built at home ran on a 240 volt socket and an assortment of extension cords strategically located throughout my house."

"Were you moving small objects short distances?"

"I guess I was."

"That's precisely the problem. We are moving large objects light years and that will require the full output of my ark's engines for a sustained period. Such a large power surge will most certainly be detected by the Aaptuuans."

"We still have to try. We're sitting ducks down here."

"Sitting what?"

"Ducks, look, never mind. You said we're under a bunch of magnetic iron. Won't that throw them off?"

"For a while, yes. No more than a couple hours. There is one more thing..."

"What is it?"

"I cannot get an exact phase match on these electronics. This may result in unpredictable behavior."

"If the only predictable outcome is I'm stuck down here the rest of my life eating cave eels then I'm ready for some unpredictability."

"As you wish. We will need to use the auxiliary power ports on the outside of the ship. The ones in here will not provide sufficient output."

Jett and Tii-Eldii moved everything outside to a large metal table. They ran a bunch of heavy cables through a network of alien devices to the power ports on the ark. Soon they had powered up the Swapper. Jett drew a large 'X' in the center of the main cavern.

"X marks the spot. Now for a test," Jett said, "this is how it works. Our current location is represented by this symbol here. This icon controls distance and this other one controls direction and dimension relative to the swapper. I can demonstrate with something small. How about Nukii?" Jett said as he placed Nukii on the table next to the swapper.

Neither of them noticed Nukii appear on the 'X' behind them while she still sat on the table where Jett had placed her. Jett activated the swapper and Nukii disappeared from both places before reappearing only on the X.

129

"It works!" Jett declared triumphantly. "Now to get home."

"Hold on, Nukii is trying to tell me something. Come here, girl, let me hold you." Tii-Eldii closed his eyes intently. She is telling me that she was in both places at once..."

"What?"

"She insists that she appeared on the 'X' before you activated the swapper."

"That's impossible..."

But before Jett could finish the sentence, Le-Wa and Chi-Col materialized in the cavern.

Jett spun around and shouted, "It's the Aaptuuans and they have a swapper!"

"Of course they do, you showed them how to build one, remember?" Tii-Eldii replied.

"Jett, you must come with us," Le-Wa ordered.

"There's no way I'm going anywhere with you again. You're going to destroy Earth!"

"We want to save your planet, Jett," Chi-Col interjected, "You must trust us."

"Why should I trust you? I've seen how you 'save' planets!"

Jett and Tii-Eldii saw themselves appear on the X behind the Aaptuuans. The second Tii-Eldii knocked Le-Wa's swapper out of his hand and it fell to the floor. The other Jett picked it up and both doubles disappeared. Without thinking Jett grabbed Tii-Eldii's tentacle and activated the swapper. They were instantly behind the Aaptuuans where they shared a quick glance before they reenacted the events they had witnessed a moment earlier. Tii-Eldii snatched up Nukii, and the three of them disappeared in a flash of light.

Jett and Tii-Eldii appeared on the deck of an Aaptuuan scout ship. They looked down on Lanedaar 3.

"Not exactly what we planned, but certainly a fortunate reversal of events," Tii-Eldii observed, "It appears phase mismatch can cause the swapper to warp the fabric of time itself causing us to be in two places at once just moments apart, fascinating..."

"Blah, blah, space time, Doctor Who - Let's get out of here! Do you know how to fly one of these things?"

"No, but there's a first time for everything."

Chapter 18
Trading Places

Craabic lay perfectly still as he watched the two strange little beings. Tii-Eldii, Nukii and the creature called Jett had disappeared, yet these two remained - confused and out of place. Craabic knew they would not easily find their way out and he decided to lay patiently in wait for one or both of them to wander in his direction. He appeared to them as a large red rock.

"Time travel. That was quite unexpected," Le-Wa said stunned.

"Not only for us," Chi-Col responded.

"Fortunately, they are trapped in orbit as the return coordinates were preset with only a single charge remaining. We will need to utilize Jett's swapper to return ourselves to the ship."

"Yes, but Jett's device is behaving unpredictably. We cannot be sure it will work as we expect."

The pair approached the testing table. They examined the quantum swapper and its power rigging.

"They were unable to recharge the battery pack, so they connected the device directly to this vehicle's power ports," Le-Wa began, "The power source itself is not entirely compatible with Aaptuuan electronics, but it can be made to cooperate. We will need to..."

With their backs turned toward him, the hungry crustacean made his move. He popped up suddenly and rushed them, his legs clicking rapidly on the rock floor.

Chi-Col turned and saw the large creature bearing

down on them. He grabbed Le-Wa by the arm, and pulled him up the ramp and into Tii-Eldii's ship.

Craabic did not give up easily. He stood on the ramp and reached into the ship as far as he could. His long clawed legs flailed about smashing into walls and controls and knocking the objects he didn't crush around the cabin with poltergeist effect. Le-Wa and Chi-Col huddled closely together under the control console.

"Another unexpected development," Chi-Col said frustrated.

"Indeed. Securing this Solarian has become quite problematic. We will wait in here until the creature settles down."

"We may be here for a while," Chi-Col observed.

In orbit, Tii-Eldii examined the Aaptuuan controls, "As you know, Jett, I have been listening to The Fold's transmissions for almost a century. In that time I have become quite fluent in their primary languages. Additionally, I have had the good fortune to intercept and analyze non-audio transmissions such as vehicle schematics. While I am not as fluent reading Aaptuuan, I do know enough to pilot this craft. Unfortunately, there appears to be a lock on the controls. It may take us some time to unlock them."

"We don't have time. The Aaptuuans will use my quantum swapper to beam themselves up here and then we're screwed."

"I don't know about that. My guess is Craabic's probably keeping them very busy at the moment," Tii-Eldii chuckled, "It was good fortune that we set the test table outside the ark. While we did not intend for Craabic to guard it,

I expect he is doing exactly that."

"Do you think Craabic ate them?"

"I do not know, but it is a highly probable outcome."

"I don't want them to get eaten. Le-Wa and Chi-Col were very good to me on Aaptuu 4."

"If that is true, then why do you run from them?"

"I want to go home."

"I can understand that."

Tii-Eldii turned his attention to the controls. He read the names of the various holographic symbols aloud as they flashed above the console, "forward shields; worm hole generator, mold casting..."

"I don't like mold casting very much," Jett interrupted, "although compared to a pocket worm, it's terrific."

"Interesting. Now where do I... ah, here it is," Tii-Eldii smiled as he swapped a couple of symbols floating above the console, "the controls are officially unlocked. Where to, Master Jett? Planet Earth?"

"Boona 4."

"What about you, Jett?"

"Once Le-Wa and Chi-Col get off this rock, they'll head straight to Earth."

"Yes, true, but The Fold will also send a contingent to Boona now that they know of me."

"What will you do then?"

"I do not know. I suppose the answer to that question depends very much on the condition of my people when we arrive there. I must examine the star charts so I can locate both Boona and Earth. We will go first to whichever is closest."

"Ok," Jett agreed.

Tii-Eldii reviewed the star chart data intensely. After some time, he pointed to a swirling holographic image of the galaxy and said, "Here we are, and here is Solaris 3. Boona 4 is here. As you can see, Boona is significantly closer to us and its current location is more or less on the way to Solaris."

Jett observed the swirling galaxy and noted that Boona was indeed somewhat on the way to Earth. Even if it weren't, it was much closer to Lanedaar at roughly twenty-five light years.

"That settles it," Jett said, "We'll go to Boona first. After we get there, you can help me figure out if Le-Wa's swapper is able to swap me to Earth. If not, are you willing to help me get home?"

"Of course, Jett. It would be my honor to return you home. Please have a seat and prepare for mold casting."

"Sweet. I can't wait," Jett said sarcastically as he plunked himself down onto the nearest chair.

Tii-Eldii methodically worked the controls. He rotated the various rings of the galaxy in four dimensions until the Lanedaar and Boona systems were in alignment. Jett saw the two systems link with a blue laser line.

"Well that's it. Get ready. Here we go," Tii-Eldii said as he sat down.

Jett braced himself. Just like during his first trip, the chair enveloped his hands, calves, and feet before encasing the rest of his body. He and Tii-Eldii shared a quick victorious glance before both were encased in metal.

"Here we go again," Jett thought to himself. He remembered his brother Jack's constant teasing, "Why can't you be more like other kids? All you want to do is sit in your room all day and play mad scientist. Why don't we head outside and play some hockey? It looks like they could use a few more players."

Why didn't he go just outside and play street hockey? After all, hockey wasn't so bad. If Jett had listened to Jack he wouldn't be hundreds of light years from home, encased in liquid metal, en route to yet another strange alien planet with an octopus man. Of course, if Jack hadn't messed with the dials and knocked Jett into the swapper, none of this would have happened. In fact, as Jett saw it, this trans-galactic nightmare was entirely Jack's fault.

"I hope they play hockey on Mars," Jett mused, "because that's where I'm going to send my stupid brother the minute I get home!"

Jett thought about his mom and wondered how she was dealing with his sudden and mysterious disappearance. Did Jack and Ravi explain what had happened? He tried to imagine the conversation, "So what you're telling me, Jack, is that your brother built a teleportation machine and disappeared into thin air?" "Yes," Jack would say, "and I certainly didn't push him into it or otherwise mess with the knobs or buttons or anything..."

Then again, Jack probably played them the video. Surely that was proof enough. Jett pictured his mother crying in the old brown leather chair his grandfather had given her. His father stood behind her with a forlorn look on his face. Their bedroom was dark with long shadows.

"Jett found my formulas. It's my fault," his mother sobbed.

"There was no way you could've known, Evelyn. He's fourteen years old. He's no theoretical physicist."

"Why couldn't he be like other teenagers? Why couldn't he be more like Jack?"

As Jett played these scenarios out in his head he couldn't help but to think that maybe his parents, his mother in particular, were actually proud of him. He did discover teleportation after all. If someone was going to capitalize on his mother's theories, why shouldn't it be him?

Jett's thoughts turned to Earth. Why was it he who had the bad luck of condemning his planet to a shadowy doom?"

"I guess the preppers were right," he thought, "If I can't save humanity, they're the best hope for our species' survival. Evolution I suppose. Survival of the best prepared."

This thought didn't comfort him at all. He pictured the rednecks who were often featured on prepper reality shows repopulating the Earth and his stomach sank. There had to be a better option. Jett would soon meet the descendants of Boona 4. Perhaps meeting the survivors of a century old neutralization would prove instructive - provided there were any survivors left to meet.

It was likely that they existed in pockets here and there. Might another Ark have already returned and set everything right? Would their stolen Aaptuuan craft fall victim to the same neutralization field that rendered all known technology inoperative?

The craft slowed dramatically. Jett's metal encasement receded and he was again sitting in a silver metal captain's chair. Tii-Eldii stared at him in a daze.

"That was something," he muttered.

"Yeah," Jett agreed, "but you get used to it."

Tii-Eldii shook his head and slowly stood up. He

approached the control panel with a slow wobbly gait and brought up a holographic image of the Boonan system.

He turned to Jett and said, "I am home. After all of these years, I am home again." Tii-Eldii paused for a moment and took it all in. "I never thought I would see it again. I hope that some have survived."

"I'm sure some have," Jett reassured.

"How can you know?" Tii-Eldii rebutted.

"I mean I hope they have."

"Yes, Jett, me too. I hope very much that they have survived the long darkness."

Tii-Eldii guided the Aaptuuan craft through the Boonan system's outer planets and satellites. The planets outside appeared desolate.

"There is no way to survive this far out without electronics," Tii-Eldii said, "the environment is too harsh to support life without artificial heat and light. They would be unable to grow crops. Many of the colonies on the outer rim relied on food imports from the inner planets. Our best hope of locating survivors is to look on the system's four inner planets. We will start with Boona 4, my home planet.

The solar system was eerily quiet. Dark empty relics of Boonan starships, satellites, and random metallic junk hung silently in space.

"These were once the busy colonies of Boona," Tii-Eldii stated heavily, "they are now empty shells, wastelands, reduced to the nothingness of eternity."

"Out, out, brief candle! Life's but a walking shadow, a poor player that struts and frets his hour upon the stage and is heard no more..." Jett trailed off.

"What is that?" Tii-Eldii asked.

"It's something my dad used to say. It's an old quote."

"What does it mean?"

"Life is fleeting... So are civilizations, societies, I suppose. Eventually we all succumb to eternity. Even the Aaptuuans. Nothing outlasts time."

"I suppose that is true," Tii-Eldii reflected. "Perhaps my people succumbed to their own time."

"Perhaps mine will, too," Jett suggested sadly.

"We Boonans have a saying," Tii-Eldii began, "The illusions we paint are the things that are real."

"You mean if you believe in something badly enough it becomes reality?"

"My people believe that the fabric of the Universe is malleable, that it is molded by the mere observation of it. Ripeem and I and other Boonan scientists employed the principals of universal malleability to create our light drive and communications equipment. These same principals dictate how I can communicate with you - through the ether of space/time."

"I suppose we all create illusions for ourselves," Jett remarked.

"No, Jett, we all create illusions of ourselves," Tii-Eldii corrected, "the how is in the way we present ourselves to The Universe. The Universe is simply a composite reflection of the thoughts that inhabit it. It is ever changing. We discovered a way to harness it for transportation and it was for this my people were neutralized."

Jett stared at the monitor. They were approaching the dark side of Boona 4 and there was nothing to suggest a

139

civilization still existed. The side of the planet facing away from the sun was dark as pitch. Jett looked at Tii-Eldii.

Tii-Eldii met his eyes and said, "Do not worry Jett. The absence of light does not confirm the absence of life. I have great hope for my people. We are a tough bunch."

Tii-Eldii guided the craft into the atmosphere in a long slow arc. With the sun at their backs, they flew out of the dusk and over a long empty plain. Soon they arrived on the outskirts of a large metropolis.

"Sidrat was once the capitol of a vast interplanetary empire," Tii-Eldii opined.

Boonans in colorful clothing stopped in their tracks and looked up in awe at the passing Aaptuuan spacecraft. Tii-Eldii set the ship down in a broad stone plaza constructed at the base of a large ziggurat. Hundreds of Boonans poured into the plaza to meet the alien craft.

"My people have survived," Tii-Eldii cried to Jett, "There is still hope for your planet."

Jett saw Tii-Eldii's joy and laughed out loud. He looked up at the monitor. The Boonans looked healthy and peaceful. Young Boonans popped in and out of the gathering masses to get a better look. The crowd formed a ring around the craft.

One pushed its way to the front of the crowd.

Tii-Eldii gasped, "Ekiwoo?"

Chapter 19
Hero's Return

Tii-Eldii left the controls, opened the ship's hatch, and raced down the gangway to Ekiwoo. The sight of a Boonan exiting the spaceship caused the crowd to breathe a collective gasp. Armed guards stepped in front of Ekiwoo and used their long serrated staffs to stop Tii-Eldii in his tracks. Jett held Nukii tightly, following a few close steps behind.

"Ekiwoo, do you not recognize me?" Tii-Eldii asked.

Ekiwoo's eyes narrowed and she examined Tii-Eldii carefully. She extended her claw tentatively and Tii-Eldii raised his own to meet it. The claws clicked together above the guards' crossed staffs and lingered. After a long awkward silence, she said, "Lower your staffs, this is my husband, Tii-Eldii. He left Boona in one of the Twelve Arks before The Great Darkness, and has returned to us. He brings news of the outside worlds."

Hushed mumbles erupted from the Boonan crowd. Surprisingly, Jett found he was able to understand a great deal of the chatter.

"Tii-Eldii the great scientist?" one asked.

"The one who discovered The Tormentors?" questioned another.

"Maybe he has a way to restore the power," suggested a third.

The guards lowered their staffs and Tii-Eldii tentatively stepped past them. He held his tentacles out in a wide splaying pattern. Ekiwoo mirrored him. One by one, the tip of each tentacle met the others in a sweeping pattern from left to right. Jett wondered if this exchange was the Boonan equivalent of a handshake or a hug or something much deeper.

"It has been so very long a time, my husband," Ekiwoo lamented, "much has changed since you and the others departed."

"Indeed," Tii-Eldii agreed, "but you have survived and so have these others."

"It is a miracle," Ekiwoo said, "Billions perished in the first few years of The Great Darkness. Those of us who remain live as our ancestors did in millennia past."

"The food and supplies I left for you were sufficient?" Tii-Eldii asked.

"Not as sufficient as your companionship," Ekiwoo replied sadly, "But they got us through the hardest times." Ekiwoo paused and continued, "Many of our family were lost."

"Who was lost?"

"Now is not the time to discuss sadness and loss suffered so long ago. Let us celebrate your return!"

Ekiwoo raised her tentacles high into the air and let out a booming bellow. The other Boonans joined in chorus and the ground beneath their feet shook. The vibration tickled Jett's calves. He giggled and dropped Nukii. Nukii hit the ground and let out a loud squeak that caught Ekiwoo's attention. She slowly lowered her tentacles and the chorus fell silent. Ekiwoo turned her attention to Jett.

"Who is your friend? Is he one of The Tormentors?"

"Tormentors? You mean the Aaptuuans? The ones who brought the darkness?"

"Yes. Is he one of them?" she pressed.

"No he is not. In fact, his people may soon be cast into

142

the darkness. He is my friend, our friend, and he is the reason I was able to return home. Ekiwoo, this is Jett. Jett, meet Ekiwoo, my wife," Tii-Eldii said proudly.

"I have heard so much about you, Ekiwoo. I am glad to make your acquaintance."

Tii-Eldii turned to Ekiwoo and repeated Jett's words.

"I just said that," Jett interjected.

Tii-Eldii turned to Jett and said patiently, "I know what you said, Jett, but Ekiwoo and the other Boonans will need some time before they can understand you as I do. Until then, I will need to translate."

"Translate? You just repeated what I said in perfect English," Jett rebutted.

"No, I did not," Tii-Eldii replied, "The time we've spent together has rewired your brain to understand Boonan as your native tongue. I have never communicated with you in a language other than Boonan. This means that you can understand Ekiwoo and the others, but they cannot understand you."

"I see," replied Jett.

Ekiwoo asked Tii-Eldii, "Is everything alright with your companion? He appears confused."

"I'm not the one who's confused," Jett said flatly.

"No, he is not confused," Tii-Eldii tersely replied mostly to Jett, "His brain is wired for Boonan as a result of the time we have spent together. I believe you will find him and his story to be of significant interest. He is trying to save his planet from The Darkness that afflicts Boona 4 and her former colonies. He can help us restore power. There is so much to tell you."

"Now," Ekiwoo commanded, "Let us prepare a banquet

for our guests. You three come with me."

Tii-Eldii wrapped a tentacle around Jett and pulled him forward. Nukii leapt into his arms. The crowd parted and they followed Ekiwoo through a large archway. Jett examined the Boonan crowd. They appeared to be thriving. The city itself, while a little worse for the wear, was clean and tidy. Somehow they survived the neutralization and perhaps the human race would, too.

"Is this how you remember it?" Jett asked Tii-Eldii.

"Yes, mostly. With the exception of transport ships absent from the sky, it is not that different."

"You will see the differences soon enough, dear husband," Ekiwoo interjected. "We work very hard to preserve that which we have since recreating much of what you see is currently beyond our technical capabilities. Reactivating the power would, of course, change that."

"Of course," Tii-Eldii agreed.

"So how do you propose we do that?" Ekiwoo pursued.

"I am not sure. I know that the Aaptuuan craft we absconded with has aboard it the equipment to re-energize Boona and potentially the colonies if we can tap into the Aaptuuan satellite network."

"Did any of our colonies survive?"

"I am not sure," Tii-Eldii replied, "We came straight here."

"Did you notice any signs of life out there?"

"I did not. Empty space wreckage is scattered everywhere, but there are no signs of life. Everything is dark."

Ekiwoo led them down a series of identical stone hallways illuminated by blue plasma torches. Now and again

144

they passed a window and Jett looked down upon the city below. It was hard for Jett to believe that such a large metropolis could have survived a neutralization and remained in such good condition.

"Your people must have really pulled together after the neutralization," Jett commented.

"He said that the Boonan people must have really pulled together after The Great Darkness," Tii-Eldii translated.

"We do not know how the other planets and colonies have gotten along since The Great Darkness was forced upon us, but on Boona, all resources were mustered for the common good. Still, many billions perished as our agricultural production and economy collapsed. We had to take to the land in order to survive. The population has stabilized and we have adjusted."

"I wonder if my people will be so fortunate."

"Jett," Tii-Eldii encouraged, "do not discount the ingenuity of humanity. It is more resilient than you believe. It too will survive The Darkness should that be its fate."

"How can you be so sure?"

"Because it is the nature of life. Your species flourished before electricity. It will survive in its absence."

Ekiwoo led them to a large open hall. In its center stood a long stone table surrounded by stools topped with bright red cushions. At the head of the table sat an ancient Boonan.

"Thaddraver," Tii-Eldii said as he took a knee and bent over reverently.

"Tii-Eldii, you have returned to us. Please sit down and tell me what goes on beyond the boundaries of our little

145

planet."

Tii-Eldii raised himself up and took a seat at the table next to Thaddraver.

"Who is your friend?" Thaddraver inquired.

"This is Jett. He found me on Lanedaar 3, the planet I took refuge on after The Great Darkness. He means to save his planet from a similar fate."

"The Tormentors seek to plunge his planet into darkness?"

"Yes, Thaddraver."

"How did he come to find you?"

"Just as our people were punished for discovering light drive, Jett's people are under scrutiny for his discovery of teleportation. He has found a method of warping space-time and simply appeared on Lanedaar 3."

"Impressive," Thaddraver commented, "Please continue."

"Jett was captured by The Tormentors, Aaptuuans as they are known throughout the galaxy, but subsequently escaped using his teleportation device. I found him wandering the deserts of Lanedaar 3. The Aaptuuans were close behind him and we narrowly escaped in one of their starships. We believe that the Aaptuuans pursuing Jett are still trapped on Lanedaar 3."

"How long before you think the Aaptuuans will arrive here to reclaim their ship and punish us further for your interference?"

"I expect they will arrive soon, within a matter of days, maybe hours, to collect Jett and their spacecraft, but I do not believe they will punish the Boonan people further."

"Why not? You have defied them."

"The Aaptuuans will not see it that way. They are not a vengeful species. It is a violation of The Ten Laws."

"If that is true, why did they destroy our civilization? Why have they subjected us to The Great Darkness for nearly a century?"

"Thaddraver, during my long absence, I monitored Aaptuuan communications almost constantly. They are a peaceful race that has been tasked with the endless chore of keeping peace in the galaxy and beyond. The Great Darkness was cast upon us because they, The Fold, viewed us as a threat to galactic peace."

"Why would they consider Boona a threat? They obviously possess far greater technology. Why not approach us and voice their concerns. Why murder billions without warning?"

"We were given a warning," Tii-Eldii replied.

"Were we?"

"Yes, we called it The Ten Laws of Civilized Living."

"Stuff of religious zealots. Those tenants are thousands of years old. That was their warning to us?"

"Yes," Tii-Eldii replied.

"You mean to say that the Aaptuuans have observed us since our early history?" Thaddraver trailed off.

"Longer still," Tii-Eldii replied softly, "They mapped our solar system 45,000 years ago and began cataloging its life 13,000 years later and have been watching us ever since. They know more about our evolution and history than we may ever know. They are currently monitoring and cataloging millions of systems, and yet they still have the resources to track us here

147

and will inevitably show up looking for their ship. That is why we cannot stay long."

"But you have just arrived," Ekiwoo interrupted.

"Yes, but I must take Jett home before they catch up with us. But before I leave, I may be able to find a way to disable the field that is inferring with our electronics."

"How will you do this?" Thaddraver asked.

"The Aaptuuan craft we traveled in is the very same model used to carry out neutralizations. It contains the control system governing the satellites that generate the disabling field. Before we depart the Boonan System, I will find a way to deactivate the field generators."

"Won't the Aaptuuans just reactivate them when they get here?" Jett chimed in.

"Not necessarily. If the Aaptuuans believe Boonans have accepted The Ten Laws, they may leave well enough alone."

"Why would they do that?" Thaddraver challenged. "We have every reason to believe they will reactivate the field the moment they arrive looking for you."

"There is a good chance they will, but there have been instances where the field has failed and The Fold has elected to give those lucky beings a second chance," Tii-Eldii paused a moment, "however, I have never heard of them granting a third chance."

"What are you saying?"

"Thaddraver, what I am saying is that if I deactivate the field generators and The Fold decides we are not ready, Boona and her colonies may never have power again. This is the decision you will have to make for Boona."

Thaddraver leaned back in his chair. He stared up at the ornate ceiling. He studied it silently for a long time. Jett looked up. The meticulously carved ceiling depicted epic battles between Boonan warriors and various other hominids in a host of settings which Jett believed to be the various planets of the Boonan system. It was the story of the Boonan Empire, a tale of bloody conquest and brutal subjugation told by the victor.

"They will not keep the power on," Thaddraver said at long last. "Do not restore it. Doing so will only bring false hope and disappointment to Boona. We need to gain their permission. How do we convince The Fold that we are ready?"

"We must adopt the Ten Laws of Civilized Living and indoctrinate them into all of our thoughts and actions. We must convince all to do this."

"Tii-Eldii, I do not need to tell you that we are a civilized people, but since your departure, necessity has forced us to live in harmony. There is no murder or theft. We no longer require a military force or police to enforce our laws. We live as equals with those we once subjugated. When they capture you, as I'm sure they will, please plead the case of your people. Please plead the case for Boona."

"You have my word, Thaddraver," Tii-Eldii promised.

"You have mine, too." Jett offered.

"Tii-Eldii, I very much like your friend," Thaddraver said, "I cannot understand what he says, but he has a positive energy. You must take him home. If you help him save his people, perhaps the Aaptuuans will look more favorably upon us."

"Certainly, Thaddraver."

"Go now and do not tell anyone else of our discussion. A feast is being prepared in your honor, and I am sure you would like to be sent off with a full belly. Go now. I will see you there shortly. Ekiwoo please escort our honored guests."

"Yes, Thaddraver," Ekiwoo answered.

Thaddraver bowed his head and left the chamber.

"He's off in a hurry," observed Jett.

"He has much to do. I am sure this news is quite a shock to him."

"Come this way," Ekiwoo motioned, "The festivities will begin shortly."

"Come, Jett, we must not be late," Tii-Eldii said.

Jett teased, "I hope there's something there for me to eat. And Nukii, too. She's hungry."

"There will be food beyond measure. Boonan feasts are something to behold, Jett!"

"Well, what are we waiting for?" Jett asked Nukii. "C'mon girl."

Nukii purred softly and rolled up Jett's leg and into his arms.

"That a girl," Jett smiled, "Let's eat!"

Jett sprinted down the corridor after Tii-Eldii and Ekiwoo.

Chapter 20
Not so Farewell

Chi-Col peered out various portal windows as he tried to determine Craabic's whereabouts. Craabic slammed a large claw into one of them and violently shook the ark. Chi-Col flew backward into the control console.

"That creature is never going to give up," Le-Wa observed as he carefully crept to another window and looked outside.

Craabic again jolted the ark. Le-Wa was thrown to the floor. When he looked up, he noticed something. Craabic's eyes, which sat perched on long tentacle-like appendages, quietly watched his and Chi-Col's every move through myriad windows around the ship.

"Look there," Le-Wa pointed, "Those black balls at the bottom of the windows are its eyes. It has been observing us."

"It is hiding beneath the ship. We must cover the windows. The creature is lying in ambush. It is trying to anticipate our next move."

The wayward Aaptuuans explored the ark. They were careful to stay clear of the open door where Craabic's hungry claws would lash in randomly from time to time. They searched for items that would be useful in blocking the giant crab's view, and gathered numerous tapestries, thin sheets of gray metal, and other large objects. One by one they covered all the windows.

Each time they covered a window, Craabic's eye would move to the next or appear suddenly in a window on the other side of the ship. Craabic rocked the ark from side to side and smashed his claws into it. He lashed at them through the open doorway, and repeatedly knocked away the items shielding the windows. It took dogged determination and unwavering patience, but the Aaptuuans eventually blocked every window.

During their search of the ark, Chi-Col found a large cylindrical spotlight stored with the spacesuits.

"What a useful device," he noted, "I would like to test a theory I have concerning a bright light's effect on subterranean eyesight."

"Excellent thesis, Chi-Col. I eagerly await your findings," Le-Wa smiled mischievously.

Left with no other way to spy on his prey, Craabic was forced to peek through the open doorway. At first, this afforded Craabic a better view of the situation. He watched the Aaptuuans as they directed a long cylindrical object toward him. A sudden blinding flash of light seared Craabic's sensitive retinas. Stunned, Craabic shrieked and retreated to the far end of the cave.

"This is the very thing we need to hold that creature at bay long enough to access the quantum exchanger and return to our ship," Le-Wa stated.

A racket of bangs and knocks rose up from outside the ship. Chi-Col walked over to one of the windows and removed a thin metal sheet. He saw Craabic spinning furiously in circles between the large red boulders. He bounced from one to the next and kicked up dust and rocks. Many of these rained down on the ark and threatened to destroy the quantum swapper.

"I think we blinded it," reported Chi-Col, "temporarily at least. We will now take advantage of the situation."

"I will position the light in the doorway. You run down

the gangway and grab the device. Bring it back inside and we will power it up in here by rerouting some circuitry."

Chi-Col agreed, "The creature is moving further away from the craft."

Craabic blundered blindly toward the lake in search of cold water. He hoped it would sooth his burning eyes. Chi-Col silently slunk down the ramp toward the quantum swapper. Upon reaching the table, he grabbed the device, the battery pack, and miscellaneous electronics that were attached to it. He never once took his eyes off Craabic who was now soaking his entire head in the lake. His shrieking ceased and left only the sound of water dripping faintly in the distance. All else was still.

Chi-Col turned toward the gangway. He did not notice the thin silver cord connecting the swapper to a series of accordion like capacitors. On his fourth step, the capacitors were pulled off the table and crashed loudly to the floor. Craabic's head sprung up and spun around. Chi-Col froze in his steps. He stared at Craabic. Craabic, still unable to see, focused intensely in the direction of the noise. Then, he rushed blindly toward Chi-Col. Chi-Col turned and ran toward the gangway while Le-Wa shined the glaring light at Craabic, but the light was of no use.

Chi-Col sprinted for the ark's door, but was suddenly stopped just short by the cord. The other end of the cord was connected to the gear that crashed to the ground. It was now snagged on the heavy table and Chi-Col could not pull it free. Worse, the cord was so strong it refused to break even as Chi-Col yanked furiously on it.

"Hurry up, the creature will be here momentarily," Le-

Wa calmly urged as Chi-Col fought with the cord. Craabic bounced from one rock to the next in a recklessly meandering course toward the ark.

"I can see that," replied Chi-Col coolly, "Maybe you can come down here and help me. For the moment anyway, the light is useless."

Le-Wa clumsily dropped it on the floor as he hurried to help his friend. Craabic, who had momentarily stopped, heard the soft clank of the flashlight and footsteps and again charged the ark.

"We must disconnect the cord," Chi-Col telepathed.

"Leave the battery," replied Le-Wa.

"We may need it."

"Yes, but we can come back for it if necessary."

Le-Wa agilely disconnected the cord as Craabic crashed into the table and sent electronics flying in every direction. The Aaptuuan battery popped out of Chi-Col's hand as the equipment it was attached to was sent hurtling across the cave.

"In the nick of time, as they say," Le-Wa commented as the two scrambled up the ramp.

Craabic, attracted to the sound of pattering feet, charged the ramp. He slammed into it and dislodged it from the doorway sending the ramp spinning off into the dark recesses of the cave. Le-Wa, who was not quite inside, fell backward into the void and onto the stunned creature.

Craabic, stunned from his collision, didn't realize Le-Wa rested in a depression in his shell. Le-Wa did his best not to move or make a sound. He communicated with Chi-Col telepathically.

"This creature has become a major impediment to our mission," he thought.

"I would have to agree," Chi-Col responded telepathically, "You need to establish a neural link to lull the creature into a restful state."

Le-Wa concurred, "It is currently my only option."

Le-Wa carefully sat up and pivoted his body around until he faced Craabic's blinded eyes. Once in position above where he believed Craabic's brain was located, he placed both of his hands gently on Craabic's cold shell and closed his eyes. Craabic, unaware of Le-Wa's presence, heard a soothing voice in his mind.

"These creatures are no threat to you or your friends. They are here to help. Leave them alone and they will leave this place forever."

"Protect. Protect. Protect," Craabic responded to the voice.

"There is nothing to protect," the voice continued, "these creatures are your friends."

"Not friends, food!"

"Not food, poison. Do not eat poisonous creatures. Help them and they will leave you and your friends alone."

"Friends gone. Must protect. Must eat."

The creature had been trained over many years to protect its master's possessions, and convincing it otherwise was a futile exercise. Le-Wa decided he needed to change his tactics.

"Chasing these pesky little creatures is exhausting," the voice in Craabic's mind lamented, "you must rest. They will be here later. Just a little rest now... Rest now... Rest..."

Craabic felt tired. These creatures were nothing but trouble. Ever since they arrived in the cave, he experienced injury after injury. The voice was right. Where would these creatures go? He would rest just outside the door. They would not dare try to escape.

"Yes, they would not dare escape. They are too afraid of you. They will still be here when you wake up," the voice consoled.

Chi-Col watched from the portal nearest the doorway. He noticed the joints in Craabic's legs relax. The giant crab's body slowly lowered itself to the ground. His eye stems bent over like wilting flowers, and his giant shell slumped to the ground. Finally, Craabic's eyes closed. Le-Wa carefully withdrew his hands and stood up.

"With the creature sedated, I will come to the doorway and pull you up," Chi-Col telepathed.

Le-Wa stepped very slowly and deliberately so as to not disturb the sleeping creature. He made his way to the door. There Chi-Col waited and lowered a cable to Le-Wa and pulled him into the ark. They closed the door and immediately went to work on the quantum exchanger.

They rerouted cables from the various power sources and combined them all into a large wire bundle. They ran this bundle into a gray metal box that Le-Wa had formed out of various items he found in the hold. The swapper plugged into this box with an adapter Le-Wa fashioned. The only other device connected to the black box was a plain yellow knob.

Once everything was ready, Le-Wa gave the order, "Power the ark."

Chi-Col flipped several switches on the console and a

156

low hum filled the ship and echoed throughout the cavern. The commotion woke Craabic who stood up with a start and spun around in confused circles. He banged on the hatch with his giant claws in earnest.

"That creature will be the end of us," Chi-Col observed.

"It's almost ready," Le-Wa responded as he fiddled with the yellow knob, "Once I sync the power phase, the machine will be fully operational and we can return to our ship."

"I am searching for our ship, but there does not appear to be any spacecraft orbiting this planet. It appears that Jett and his friend have stolen our ship."

"Likely to return to Fabboett or Solaris 3. We will need to return to Aaptuu 4 and alert The Fold," Le-Wa offered.

The ark again shook violently as Craabic banged on the hull outside. Sparks flew from the electronics.

"Recalibrating jump to The Garden of the High Council," Chi-Col reported, "The power is sufficient for one jump at a time."

"You go first. I will join you there," Le-Wa said as Craabic slammed into the ark again and threw him to the floor. The power flickered off and on.

Le-Wa stood up and returned to the yellow knob. "OK," he said, "It is ready."

Chi-Col stepped up to the device and placed his hands on the black sensor pad. Le-Wa initiated the jump and with a flash of light, Chi-Col was gone - and so was the quantum exchanger!

Le-Wa stared at the empty spot while Craabic continued his assault until he violently upended the ark and sent everything flying. Le-Wa slammed into the ceiling. Everything went black.

Chapter 21
Into the Fire

Jett watched Tii-Eldii and Ekiwoo get reacquainted. Their interaction was touching and Jett didn't want to be the reason Tii-Eldii left her again. He was fairly certain he could make the jump to Earth using the Aaptuuans' swapper, so long as he could draw sufficient power from the spacecraft. Jett watched the hordes of Boonans celebrate Tii-Eldii's return, for he brought renewed hope to their planet, their civilization, and they rejoiced! Boonans old and young were drawn to the strange creature called Jett, and he was surrounded by gawking onlookers.

"How does it manage with only four appendages?" one asked.

"Does it understand what we say?" questioned another.

"What does it eat?" inquired a youngling.

"What is that creature it's holding? Do you suppose it's edible?" another asked licking its beak.

"No you can't eat HER," Jett shouted, "Stay away from her!" Jett squeezed Nukii in his arms and she purred, burrowing deeper into his arms.

"Sounds like the little fuzz ball is dying."

"Horrible!" several said together.

"Enough of this!" Ekiwoo commanded. "This creature, Jett, is our guest. Grant him the same courtesy you would grant me. I expect no less."

"Of course, Ekiwoo," said one.

"My apologies, I did not mean to offend," offered

another.

"Make no more apologies. Instead make merry. This day we celebrate Tii-Eldii's return and the hope it brings our people."

The crowd cheered and raced off to join in the festivities. Ekiwoo ordered a contingent of guards to keep the looki-loos at bay. The guards formed a circle around Jett and discouraged unauthorized visitors from getting too close.

Their presence did nothing to stop the chatter though. Jett saw clusters of Boonans huddled in small groups throughout the crowd. They gawked and motioned in his direction.

"I must be quite something to them," Jett said to himself, "as strange to them as they are to me, maybe even stranger."

Once the guards were stationed around Jett, Ekiwoo turned her full attention to Tii-Eldii. It wasn't long before they lost interest in him altogether.

Jett cautiously nibbled his food. It was alkaline and metallic tasting and otherwise unappealing. Eventually, he found something that tasted like mashed potatoes. He managed to get down a little bit of that, but Jett mostly sipped his water and waited for an opportunity to sneak back to the ship.

A band struck up a lively tune. The Boonan hordes cheered and danced raucously. Several rushed the head table and lifted Tii-Eldii and Ekiwoo from their seats. They carried the two dignitaries to the center of the crowd and raised them onto a large platform. There they led the crowd in a wild dance of flailing tentacles and cheerful hoots.

160

Soon the guards joined the fun and he found himself sitting alone and unnoticed. Jett surreptitiously slunk under the table and he and Nukii disappeared into the shadows. To his surprise, no one followed. Soon the din of the party faded and Jett made a b-line for the Aaptuuan ship. The maze of alleyways and tunnels were virtually identical. Jett searched for points he might recognize as he went, but saw nothing familiar and was soon lost. He wandered about aimlessly. Light from the blue plasma torches cast long shadows that danced eerily about. The celebration was no longer audible.

At the feast, Tii-Eldii reveled in his reunion with Ekiwoo. Time had indeed caused his heart to grow fonder and his long absence gave him a deep appreciation for both Ekiwoo and the traditions of his people. Tii-Eldii was elated and he had Jett to thank, but when he looked to the head table to invite Jett to join the fun, he was not there. Tii-Eldii scanned the buffet and the dance floor. Jett was gone.

Tii-Eldii's tentacles dropped and he rushed to the head table. Ekiwoo's eyes followed him with concern, and she noticed that neither Jett nor the guards were where she had left them. Ekiwoo ran after Tii-Eldii. She summoned guards as she went.

"He's gone," Tii-Eldii said in a panic.

"Where would he go?" Ekiwoo asked.

"He's gone to the ship!" Tii-Eldii exclaimed.

"Guards," Ekiwoo called, "find the Solarian and return him to me. Do not harm him. Go! Now!"

A dozen Boonan guards carrying long staffs hustled to the Aaptuuan ship.

161

"We will wait here," Ekiwoo said, "I do not wish to call attention to the Solarian's disappearance. My officers will return him shortly. He could not have gone far."

"He plans to jump to Solaris. Forgive me, wife," he clamored and raced after the guards.

"Tii-Eldii, wait!" Ekiwoo pleaded.

Jett, meanwhile, found himself hopelessly lost. Exhausted, he leaned hard against a cold stone wall and slunk to the ground. His head fell to his knees.

"I'm hopeless. 9.5 billion people counting on me and I can't even find my way back to the stupid spaceship."

Jett felt something nudge his right foot. He lifted his head and saw Nukii rolling frantically back and forth. She chirped excitedly.

"You know where the ship is, girl?"

Nukii purred and rolled back in the direction from which Jett had just come.

"The ship's not that way, girl."

Nukii stopped; bounced up and down wildly; and resumed her trajectory.

"You're leading me back to the party. Better than being lost, I suppose."

Jett wearily rose to his feet and ran after her. After a few dozen meters, Nukii darted through a narrow opening between two tall buildings.

"There he is!" shouted the dark profile of a Boonan Guard.

"Oh, great," Jett muttered looking through the narrow opening. "I don't know about this, Nuke's. Looks pretty tight in there."

Jett lifted his arms over his head and squeezed himself into the claustrophobic gap. Nukii was a few meters ahead of him. She rolled easily through and out the far side. The guard ran to the gap and reached several tentacles in after Jett.

"Stop," he shouted, "You are going to wedge yourself in there and we'll never get you out. Please return to the party with me. You have nothing to fear."

"Give Tii-Eldii my best. Thank him for everything he's done for me," Jett shouted as his right arm reached the far side.

More guards converged on the opening. Several raced around to intercept Jett on the other side. A long tentacle wrapped itself around Jett's ankle.

"Got you!" the guard trumpeted. His grip on Jett's ankle was fierce.

"Let me go!"

Jett looked up as he strained to escape. He saw the gleaming Aaptuuan scout ship just a few meters away.

"Sooooo close. Ugh..."

Nukii rolled briskly past Jett.

"Where are you going, girl? The ship's that way!"

She approached the tentacle, paused briefly, and then let out a high pitched squeal. Translucent slime sprayed out from her body. The slime seared the tentacle.

"AHHHHHH!" the guard screamed retracting it.

Jett popped out of the gap like a champagne cork, and landed face first in the plaza. His shin was on fire. Some of the caustic slime had sprayed onto his leg and it ate a hole through his gown. He shed the steaming garment and ran naked across the plaza toward the ship to the clanking of dog tags.

"He's over there!" one of the guards called to the others.

Jett and Nukii ran up the gangway, and closed the hatch. Jett grabbed the swapper and connected it to the ship's power output, and its screen lit up.

"Looks like we're in business, girl!"

The Aaptuuans had made several remarkable improvements to his invention. The most useful of these was a neural user interface. By simply thinking about Earth and its solar system, the GPS was able to locate it and program the coordinates. Jett was astounded. Maybe if he envisioned his home he could go there directly. Jett remembered each detail of his house, the property it sat on, and the surrounding neighborhood, sure enough the galactic positioning system located his house in San Jose, California.

"I'm loving this intergalactic GPS! Well, here goes nothing. You coming, girl?" Jett asked Nukii and she rolled up Jett's leg and into his waiting arms.

He pressed the 'exchange' button just as the ship's hatch door dropped open and Tii-Eldii rushed in. A green blue field enveloped Jett, but before he disappeared he smiled and waved to Tii-Eldii.

"Thank you for..." but before Jett could finish his sentence, he disappeared in a flash of light and puff of smoke.

"No, thank you Jett," Tii-Eldii replied, "I am forever in your debt."

"Boona is forever in your debt," Ekiwoo added, "Perhaps we will see him again one day."

"I hope you are right."

Chapter 22
Can't Find My Way Home

This swap felt much longer than he anticipated. Jett fell endlessly into a dark abyss, and just when he thought the swap would never end, he found himself standing naked in his own backyard, Nukii cradled in his arms. The familiar smells of cedar and eucalyptus filled his nose. Jett knew this was no illusion. He was finally home and the lights were on inside.

"Thank God, we're here," Jett told Nukii stumbling awkwardly up the back steps.

Jett opened the screen door and turned the knob, but the door was locked. Without a stitch of clothing, Jett clung to the shadow of the house and made his way to the front yard.

"Sorry, girl," Jett apologized as he reached the front porch and used Nukii to cover his privates, "The family jewels aren't meant to be seen by the neighbors, if you know what I mean."

With his front covered, Jett broke a branch off a nearby banana palm and used it to cover his behind.

"That should do it. Ok, Nukes, time to meet my family."

Jett ascended the stairs quickly hoping he would not be spotted. He peeked in the living room window. The television was on. His family lounged about on the large sectional sofa as a beer commercial blared on the theater system.

Jett took one large sideways step to the front door and slowly turned the knob. He gingerly nudged it open, but it seemed the slower it moved the louder it creaked.

"Just a little more," he whispered softly to himself, "almost there..."

"Woof, woof, woof, woof, woof, woof!" Stanford barked loudly.

"Who's there?" demanded Jett Sr.

"Don't worry, dad, it's just me," Jett answered stepping into the light of the entryway.

"Jett?" Evelyn exclaimed rushing into the foyer, "Where have you been? What happened to your clothes? No matter, at least you're safe!"

Evelyn wrapped her arms around Jett and squeezed him tightly.

"Hi, mom. I missed you too. Everything is fine. If you let me get dressed, I'll explain everything."

"What happened to you? Were you visiting a nudist colony? We all thought you were dead," Jack said.

"Yeah, no thanks to you!" Jett shot back.

"What did I do?" Jack asked innocently.

"You know exactly what you did, Jack! You messed up my quantum swapper. You transported me to the upper stratosphere and I would have plummeted to my death if not for the Aaptuuans."

"The who?" his mother asked.

"Never mind. Look give me a minute to get dressed please."

"Are you sure you're all right, Jett," asked his father.

"I'm naked and very, very hungry. Other than that, I'm about as good as I could be considering what I've been through."

"Get dressed, Jett. I'll fix you something to eat."

"Thanks, mom," Jett said as he bolted upstairs.

"What's the deal with the red pompom, fairy boy?"

Jack continued wiping away the tears of relief, joy, fear, and guilt that had swept over him.

"That's enough out of you, Jack!" Jett Senior ordered, "Your brother has been missing for months. One more comment out of you and I'll send YOU to the upper stratosphere!"

"Yes, sir," Jack shrugged meekly.

Months? Had he really been gone for months? It certainly didn't feel that way to Jett. He could string together maybe a week at the most. One day traveling to Aaptuu 4, a couple of days there, before Ciallore, and then a couple more days on Lanedaar 3, followed by not quite two days on Boona. A week maybe, not months. How many months he wondered? If he had really been missing for months, did the swapper warp his ability to comprehend the passage of time?

Jett ducked into his bedroom and placed Nukii into an empty guinea pig cage.

"It's a little tight, but I need you to wait here quietly. Ok, girl?"

Nukii chirped excitedly.

"Good Nukes. Good girl," Jett encouraged as he stroked her fur lovingly.

Jett was dressed and sitting at the kitchen table in a matter of minutes. He shoved food into his mouth as fast as he could swallow it.

"Whoa, slow down there champ, chew your food," Jett Senior cautioned, "no sense choking to death."

"Leave Jett alone, he's obviously starving!" Evelyn shot back.

"It's ok, Mom. It's just that I haven't eaten any Earth

food since I left Aaptuu 4."

"Earth food? Aaptuu 4? Next stop, nut house," Jack commented.

"Enough, Jack!" Evelyn ordered.

"It's ok," Jett interjected, "I know it sounds crazy, but you have to listen to me."

Jett's family took in his story of alien abductions, The Ten Laws, the Fold, and cities on far away worlds. He told them of his chance meeting with Tii-Eldii and his journey inside the pocket worm. He described Boona and how he wanted to spare Tii-Eldii any further heartache and how he swapped himself back to Earth (known throughout the galaxy as Solaris 3) using the stolen Aaptuuan quantum swapper so he could save the human race from impending doom.

"That's quite a wild story, Jett, are you sure that's what *really* happened?" his mother asked skeptically.

"Yes, I'm sure. I was there."

"I'm sure it *seemed* like you were there," his father offered.

"Don't patronize me. I'm not crazy."

"I think Jett's seriously lost his marbles," Jack teased.

"Oh yeah, I'll prove it! Come with me," Jett called racing out of the kitchen and up the stairs.

His family followed him into his bedroom, where he stood holding Nukii and the Aaptuuan swapper.

"See," he said.

"See what? A fuzzy red pompom and a Star Trek toy?" Jack taunted.

"You of anyone should believe me, Jack. You saw the Lego experiment. You saw me disappear. This is Nukii. She is a

Lanedaarian Bush Bunny."

"A what?" asked Evelyn.

"A Lanedaarian Bush Bunny. She's quite friendly. See." Nukii rolled out of Jett's hand; down his leg; and across the floor.

"Oh my God, it's alive!!" Jett Senior exclaimed.

"Of course it is."

"So what you're telling us is this creature is from another planet," Evelyn clarified.

"Yes. Nukii is from a planet known as Lanedaar 3. It's very far from Earth, but with the swapper, it may as well be downtown San Francisco. Problem is that this invention of mine has the human race in a bit of trouble with The Fold since humans, Solarians as we're known, are so 'unstable' and 'unpredictable' and basically can't be trusted to play nicely with ourselves or others."

"Trusted by whom?" Jett Sr. pressed.

"The Fold. Look it's complicated, ok? I don't have time to explain everything to you right now. I need to get to the White House."

"The White House? That doesn't make any sense."

"Really, mom? Then how do you explain Nukii?"

"Remote control fuzz ball?" Jack offered.

"Nukes, come girl," Jett called.

Nukii rolled across the floor, up Jett's left leg, and into his arms. Once she was settled in, Jett grabbed the swapper out from under his arm and held it out in front of him.

"Crazy story, huh?" he asked, "Maybe this will convince you that I'm telling the truth."

Jett closed his eyes and the swapper's screen buzzed

169

on. Nukii chirped wildly.

"Jett, what are you doing?" Evelyn pleaded, "Stop it, you're scaring me!"

"Bye, mom," Jett replied with an uneven smirk and vanished in a flash of light.

"I've already told you, the United States does not negotiate with terrorists," President Montoya huffed slamming his fist on his desk, "it never has and I'm not about to change that."

"But sir, the intelligence is credible. There is a high likelihood that..." one of the staffers started as the Oval Office was blanketed in a flash of blinding light. Jett suddenly stood in middle of the room.

"Sorry to barge in," he apologized, "but I have to speak with President Montoya."

"Who are you? How did you get in here?" The President demanded.

"Mr. President, sir, I have a message for the people of Earth from The Fold."

Secret Service agents surrounded Jett. More poured in through the large doors, guns drawn. Others chattered feverishly into their headsets.

"Let him speak," President Montoya ordered, "holster your weapons. He's just a boy."

"Thank you, umm, Mr. President, sir. My name is Jett Javelin. I'm from San Jose, California. My mother is a theoretical physicist and I used her research papers to invent a device that can move matter through space time. I have a version of it here. It's how I got into your office." Jett held the device up so that the President could see it.

"This is Nukii. She is a creature from the planet Lanedaar 3 which is located many hundreds of light years from Earth."

"Kid, I'm sorry, but we have urgent matters of national security to deal with, we don't have time for your sci-fi fantasies. I don't know how you got in here, but you'll be sent home to your parents after you've been properly interrogated."

"No wait! I can prove it. Nukes, show them what you can do."

Nukii rolled down Jett's body and across the floor toward The President. The Secret Service agents drew their guns but before they could take a shot, Nukii had rolled up onto President Montoya's desk and stopped directly in front of him. The President looked at the little red ball in disbelief. He looked up at Jett.

"Go ahead. Check her out," Jett urged, "You'll see she's very much alive and very much not from Earth."

President Montoya held his hand up to the agents and signaled them to hold their positions. He carefully examined Nukii. The President reached out to touch her, and Nukii rolled forward and purred. Startled, the President lurched back in his chair.

"Well, I don't know what this thing is, but it's certainly unique. Where did you say it's from?"

"Lanedaar 3."

"Lanedaar 3," President Montoya repeated, "and where exactly is that?"

"It's on the far side of the Boonan system."

"I see. And you've been to Lanedaar 3?"

"Yes, and to Boona and Aaptuu 4 and Ciallore."

"And you went there with this teleportation device of yours?"

"Yes, sir. Most of them, anyway…"

"Let me have a closer look at your device. Gentlemen, let him through."

The agents made a narrow pathway for Jett. He approached the President's desk and placed the swapper next to Nukii. Nukii rolled back into Jett's arms. He hugged her and she purred loudly.

"That thing really likes you."

"We've been through a lot together, sir."

President Montoya picked up the strange alien device and turned it over in his hands.

"You made this?"

"No, I did not. It's an Aaptuuan version."

"Aaptuuan?"

"Yes, sir, the Aaptuuans based this device on my original version."

"Sir," an aid interrupted, "we've reviewed the video footage. This boy actually *materialized* in your office. There is no explanation how he did it."

"I did it with the quantum swapper."

"If that's true, our friend Jett here may have solved some of our most pressing national security issues," President Montoya smiled.

"No, you can't use it for that. They won't allow it!" exclaimed Jett, "You'll condemn us all!"

"I'm the President of the United States. Who are you to tell me what I can and can't do? You appear out of thin air in my office with a technology that holds unfathomable scientific and military potential and you tell me I can't use it?"

"I'm sorry, sir, but if you use it for any purpose that violates The Ten Laws, they'll neutralize Earth!"

"Who will neutralize Earth?"

"The Fold."

"And where is this Fold?"

"Everywhere and always," Jett answered quietly, "They will be here soon. They are looking for me. We don't have much time."

"Much time to do what?"

"To change. To follow The Ten Laws. To lay down our weapons."

"Take him and his creature below along with the machine. He doesn't leave here until I figure out how he got in and what kind of animal that is."

"Wait!" Jett screamed desperately, "You don't understand. They'll be here anytime! They're looking for me!"

"Get him out of here," President Montoya ordered.

Agents grabbed Jett by both arms and jostled Nukii free. She fell to the ground and rolled out through the open double doors and into the White House.

"Go, girl! Get outta here!" Jett called after her.

"Catch that thing!" President Montoya shouted.

Jett was wrestled out of the Oval Office and into an elevator that descended into the depths of the White House complex. Nukii raced down the long hallway until she found an ornate vent in the wall. She pushed herself against it as Secret

Service agents closed in on her. She contorted her body and managed to press herself through one of the grill's openings, squeezing through just as an agent's gloved hand closed on her fur and tore a chunk out.

Nukii screeched in pain. Her cries echoed through the air ducts with such ferocity that it interrupted President Montoya and his staff.

"What the hell was that?" The President asked.

Nukii, frightened and lost, set off to find Jett.

Meanwhile, on Lanedaar 3, a contingent of Aaptuuan scouts pulled Le-Wa's unconscious body from the wreckage of the Boonan Ark while a frustrated Craabic looked on from the far side of a protective energy field. Chi-Col placed his hand on Le-Wa's forehead. He looked up at the others in silence as they solemnly carried Le-Wa to the staging area. Now that Le-Wa was secured, Chi-Col and his new partner, Nomika, were off to Solaris 3 where they hoped to capture Jett before he caused any more trouble.

Chapter 23
Truth be Told

Jett was taken to a brightly lit room and strapped to a cold metal chair. Cameras observed him from every angle. A large framed mirror graced the wall directly opposite him. The room matched every interrogation scenario he had seen on TV and in the movies.

All but two of the agents left. The last one out gently closed the door and locked it from the outside.

"Classic good cop, bad cop," Jett thought, "I'll just sit tight until the Aaptuuans show up and neutralize everything."

"Hi, Jett, I'm Agent Matheson and this is Agent Walker. We're going to ask you a few questions."

"I suspected as much," Jett replied smartly.

"How did you get into The Oval Office?" Agent Matheson started.

"I already told you. I used the Quantum Swapper."

"You used the Quantum Swapper. Can you explain to Agent Walker and me how, exactly, a Quantum Swapper works?"

"Look I don't have time to give you a lesson in Quantum Mechanics, the Aaptuuans will be here any minute. They'll take me back to Tower 100 and I'll be stuck talking to Bob and eating endless amounts of Grammy's lasagna, while the Aaptuuans complain I'm shouting telepathically. The two of you and everyone else will be left here in the dark. Lights out. Game over. Bye-bye."

"Slow down, son," Agent Walker said, "Why don't you start from the beginning and tell us everything?"

"Ok," Jett agreed, "It's not like I'm going anywhere, and you probably won't believe me anyway, but here goes nothin'," he said pulling on his restraints, "It all started with my mom's papers on quantum particle exchange..."

Nukii rolled furiously through the White House's ducting system anxiously searching for Jett. Outside, the agents pulled all of the furniture away from the walls in an effort to locate and monitor every ventilation grate, but deep in the bowels of the White House Nukii found plenty of unguarded grates and empty rooms. She explored the seemingly endless labyrinth until, she heard what she thought was Jett's voice. She stopped and listened intently.

Nukii rolled slowly toward the sound trying to zero in on where it was coming from. Jett's voice grew louder until Nukii discovered the room where Jett was being held.

She purred softly at the sight of her friend. However, the vent was far too small for her to squeeze through it, and based on her experience thus far, this vent simply would not do.

Nukii took to exploring the network of ducts that encircled the interrogation room until she finally found a grate large enough to accommodate her. She emerged from the duct onto a high metal shelf. Nukii looked down onto the room below. She saw many agents and scientists gathered in front of a window that looked out on Jett.

She rolled cautiously to the edge of the shelf, and carefully dropped onto the shelf below her, but her weight overwhelmed it and caused it to give way. A loaded pistol hit the corner of a desk and fired a single shot into the large fluorescent light above the spectators. Glass and sparks rained down everywhere. The door swung open abruptly and a female agent rushed in.

She held Nukii firmly in her hands and announced, "We caught his little friend. We're going to take it to the lab. This thing caused quite a ruckus in the observation room... knocked a loaded pistol to the floor."

"Nukii!" Jett exclaimed, "Come here, girl!"

"I don't think so," Agent Walker ordered, "Get it out of here, Agent Wilcox."

Determined to be reunited with Jett, she sprayed slime all over Agent Wilcox's hands and forearms. The caustic concoction began to dissolve Wilcox's suit sleeves and seared her skin.

"Ahhhhhhhh!" she screamed and threw Nukii to the floor. Agent Wilcox sprinted into the bathroom and tore off her tattered jacket, and washed the burning slime off of herself. The hair on her arms was completely burned off and her skin was firetruck red. She stood there awkwardly in her bra and slacks.

"Here, put this on?" Agent Matheson offered handing her a white lab coat.

"Thanks," she said, "That stuff it spits out or shits out burns something fierce. We'll need some kind of glass cage to keep it in once we catch it."

"Hey, Nukes. Great to see you girl. How'd you find me?"

Nukii purred and rubbed herself on Jett's legs like a friendly tabby cat.

"There it is, catch it!" Agent Wilcox shouted through the doorway and was now joined by several fresh agents. Agent Walker shut the door behind them trapping Nukii inside.

"Wait!" Jett shouted, "I'll give her if you promise you won't hurt her."

"Everyone stop," Agent Walker ordered, "Jett, what is it you need us to do?"

"For starters, I need everyone to back off. Then you need to untie my hands so I can pick Nukii up off the floor and calm her down. Once she's chilled out, I'll carry her to whichever laboratory you'd like."

"Do as he says," Agent Walker ordered.

The cadre of agents backed away from Jett and lined up against the wall. Agent Walker undid Jett's restraints, and Jett snagged Nukii.

"There, there, girl. It's ok. These nice gentlemen would like to have a closer look at you is all. Let's not give them any more trouble, ok?"

Nukii emitted a low growl.

Jett turned to Agent Walker and said, "She doesn't like you or your men very much."

"No matter," he replied flatly, "Let's bring her down to the lab."

"Ok," Jett reluctantly agreed. He stood up and walked to the door.

Agent Matheson waited on the other side along with several agents and scientists.

"Jett has agreed to escort his little friend to the lab. I'll go with him. The rest of you can wait here," Agent Walker said.

He guided Jett down the brightly lit hallway.

Maintenance staff rushed past them to fix the broken light in the observation room. They soon left the bustle of the interrogation rooms behind them and were completely alone. Agent Walker ordered Jett to stop in front of a door labeled simply: Biohazard Lab.

"Nukii's not a Biohazard!" Jett argued defiantly.

"She is until we determine otherwise. You agreed to bring her here and I promise she won't be harmed. Then we can sit down again and finish our conversation," Agent Walker said as he pressed his hand on the door's biometric scanner. The door popped open with a hiss.

"After you," Walker urged.

Jett entered the room. It was a large, well equipped laboratory. He knew that if he left Nukii, there was a high likelihood she would be dissected or worse. Agent Walker closed the door behind them.

"Hello, Jett," a familiar voice echoed in Jett's mind.

"Chi-Col?" Jett asked out loud as Chi-Col appeared behind Agent Walker.

"Excuse me," Agent Walker replied thinking the Jett was talking to him.

"Remember all that stuff I was telling you before, Agent Walker?"

"Yes, what about it?"

"Well, that's an Aaptuuan," Jett said pointing to Chi-Col.

Agent Walker turned around and gasped. There stood a chalk white alien with large black eyes and a short chubby body. He tried to draw his gun, but couldn't move a muscle. He was frozen in place.

"There, there, Agent Walker" Chi-Col telepathed, "You do not need to use your weapon."

"I do not need to use my weapon," he parroted with a distant look in his eyes.

"We will be out of your way momentarily. The boy and his creature will cause you no further trouble."

"They will cause me no further trouble," he repeated.

"I'm not going with you!" Jett said to Chi-Col.

"I am afraid you have no choice in the matter, Jett. We must return you to Aaptuu 4. Dr. VaaCaam-a has requested your presence."

"Not before I can warn Earth of what's to come."

"Consider Earth sufficiently warned. As we speak, they are recording our interaction. It will serve as proof you are telling the truth. What they choose to do with this information will determine their fate and the fate of your planet."
Jett turned to run, but it was fruitless. He couldn't move.

"Let me go!" Jett demanded, but Chi-Col ignored him and in a bright flash of light Jett, Nukii, and Chi-Col vanished.

Agent Walker finished the motion of drawing his gun, but found himself all alone in the laboratory. He looked around confused. The lab door flew open and a dozen agents rushed in with weapons drawn, but Jett and Nukii were gone.

"I want this entire facility locked down!" Agent Matheson ordered, "Take Agent Walker to medical immediately! He may be contaminated!"

Back in the observation room's sink, what was left of Agent Wilcox's slimed shirt vibrated erratically. Dozens of small marble sized red balls emerged from underneath it.

The miniature bush bunnies frantically scurried about the sink basin. One by one, they popped up onto the counter, fell to the floor, and rolled off in every direction. A few were attracted to a white lab coat that hung nearby. They climbed the coat and nibbled at it, emitting soft chirps that got the attention of the others. Soon all of the baby bush bunnies happily and thoroughly consumed the lab coat.

In no time, they ate the remaining lab coats, paper towels, toilet paper, and toilet seat covers. The bathroom door swung open and a man carrying a newspaper walked in.

The bush bunnies sped off into the dark corners of the bathroom to hide. The man went into one of the stalls and closed the door behind him. The bunnies watched as the man's feet changed direction. He dropped his pants to his ankles, and the nearest bush bunny rolled over to the man's crumpled pants and nibbled on them tentatively.

The others followed suit and quietly swarmed the stall, quickly going to work on the man's slacks. He felt a tickling sensation on his ankles. He looked down to see all that remained of his pants were the zipper and a single metal button resting on the floor between his feet. Several red balls happily munched on what was left of his pants. One nibbled tentatively on his shoe lace.

He sprung up and called out, "The red ball creature is in here with me, only there's lots of them now and they've eaten my pants!"

The man's booming voice frightened the bush bunnies, and they raced out of the stall in every direction. Several agents rushed into the bathroom. Bush bunnies rushed outside and into the hallway and sped off at tremendous velocity. Agent Walker emerged on the scene.

"Where did all these creatures come from? I thought there was only one!" he demanded. "Secure this bathroom before any more of them escape. You three, contain those," he ordered pointing down the hall.

But catching bush bunnies is no easy task. They are unusually fast and genetically programmed to spray highly acidic and impossibly sticky goo at predators. Worse, these were still small enough to escape through any grate, drain, or gap in the wall. In all, Agent Walker's men managed to capture only eleven of the creatures. Many of the agents suffered severe burns to their hands and arms that required immediate medical attention.

Dozens, maybe hundreds of the creatures emerged from the plumbing and ate every piece of fabric, paper, or plant in their path.

In orbit with Jett and Nukii sedated, The Aaptuuans prepared their return to Aaptuu 4.

"The locusts of Lanedaar 3 multiply uncontrollably," Chi-Col observed.

"It is the Solarians' own aggressive nature that causes them to do so," Nomika replied.

"A parable in the making," Chi-Col continued, "and to think, Jett was so concerned about neutralization that he never imagined a scenario like this."

"And yet, here it is. If the Solarians can't contain the bunny infestation, there will be nothing left to neutralize."

Chapter 24
The Tinkerer's Quandary

"Wake up, Jett," a gentle voice urged.

"Just a few more minutes. I have a terrible headache," Jett answered groggily.

"I have just the thing to fix up that headache of yours," the voice encouraged, "It's time to get up. There's a big day ahead."

"Big day? What's so big about today?" Jett grumbled.

"Today is the day you testify in front of the Aaptuuan High Council, of course. How could you forget something as important as that?"

Jett's eyes went wide as he shot out of bed. He looked around his room. There was his bed and everything appeared to be in its proper place: his desk, his computer, his 3D printer, everything except... *the patio door...*

"Ugh, they got me..." Jett muttered when he realized he was back in Tower 100, "Bob?"

"Yes, Jett. Did you miss me?"

"Um, a little I guess. It's good to hear a friendly voice. When did I arrive on Aaptuu 4?"

"Several hours ago. Since you were unwilling to return peacefully, you were sedated. The cup on your end table contains an herbal remedy that will alleviate any lingering discomfort."

Jett looked to his left. There was a small Dixie sized cup waiting for him on the end table. He picked it up and examined its contents. Inside was an odorless red fluid that sloshed lazily around when he swirled it.

Jett lifted the cup to the disembodied Bob and said, "Folk remedy, huh? What the heck, here's to you, Bob, my only friend in Oonuua," then shot the stuff back like a seasoned frat boy.

"You have many friends in Oonuua, Jett," Bob stated.

"Oh, yeah, like who?"

"Like Le-Wa and Chi-Col. Dr. VaaCaam-a is also quite fond of you."

"Ok, three friends and I guess you make four."

"In Oonuua one friend is all you need."

"How's that work?"

"They will explain everything to you in a short while. Can I offer you something to eat? Your grandmother's lasagna perhaps?"

"And a Dr. Pepper."

"Of course. They are waiting for you on the terrace."

The patio doors slid open. Jett climbed out of bed and walked to the table. His clothes were replaced by a soft flowing robe that caressed his body as he walked. He ran his hand down the front of it. It was the softest fabric he had ever felt.

"It's nice isn't it?" Bob commented, "It's woven from the silk of the Trophy Spider of Aaptuu 5."

"Yes, it's very nice. They're not planning to bury me in this getup are they?"

"Why would the Council wish to bury you?"

"Never mind, bad joke," Jett replied as he sat down to eat.

"I do not wish to rush you, Jett, but Chi-Col and Nomika will be here to fetch you shortly."

"Nomika? What happened to Le-Wa?"

184

"I'm afraid Le-Wa did not fare so well on Lanedaar 3. Nomika has been assigned in his place."

"What do you mean? Is he ok?"

"He is being cared for, but his injuries are critical. The creature in the cavern did quite a job on him."

"You mean Craabic? Craabic hurt Le-Wa?"

"Yes, quite seriously I'm afraid. Chi-Col will fill you in on the details when he arrives."

"I never meant to hurt him. I just wanted to get home."

"Unintended consequences born of our actions can be the most egregious consequences of all."

Jett dropped his fork, "I feel terrible. Chi-Col must be so angry with me..."

"I am not angry with you, Jett. You did precisely what you were meant to do."

"Chi-Col?"

"My apologies, Jett, I should have announced your guests," Bob interrupted.

"Chi-Col, how is Le-Wa? Is he expected to make it?"

"If by 'make it', you mean 'live', yes. He will make a full recovery. He is very fortunate. Had our team been delayed another moment, Le-Wa would no longer be with us."

"It's my fault. I left you there with Craabic. I..."

"Did what you had to do. Nothing will change that now. Finish your meal so we may go to The Council Garden."

"I'm not hungry."

"As you wish. Let us be off then."

Jett stood up and was escorted out into the long featureless hallway.

"Remember, Jett, you have friends here," Bob said as

the door silently closed behind them.

Jett didn't reply. He knew the fate of Earth rested on him, and that every one of the creatures in the council chamber could read his thoughts. He looked over at Chi-Col. Chi-Col knowingly returned his gaze.

"You're reading my thoughts right now, aren't you?"

"We can't help it," telepathed Nomika, "you think *so* loudly."

"Excuse me?" Jett replied insulted.

"Nomika is correct, Jett. Your emotions cause your thoughts to shout."

"Shout? Again, I'm just thinking," Jett said out loud.

"No, Jett, that is talking," Chi-Col corrected, "You are shouting telepathically. Strong emotions amplify your thought waves. We can not only read your mind, we also *feel your emotions*. If you are able to quiet your emotions, you will quiet your mind, and in that quiet mind, you will find the answers you seek. I suggest you begin by taking long deep breaths and counting backward from ten."

"You sound like my mom's yoga teacher."

"He must be a very wise Solarian," Nomika offered.

"She, um, yes, I suppose," Jett replied with a sideways glance.

Jett did as Chi-Col said. Beginning at ten, he took deep slow breaths all the way down to zero. When he finished, he felt a little better.

"It is a tremendous burden, but you wear it well," Chi-Col encouraged.

"Thanks, I think..."

"Indeed you do," Nomika offered, "especially

considering your firsthand knowledge of neutralization."

"Seeing what it meant for the Boonans gives me some hope regardless of the outcome."

"Your positive outlook embodies much of what we admire about your species. If only all Solarians shared your positivity."

"Positivity? Billions may soon die! I'm about as positive as anyone can be considering the circumstances."

"Positive nonetheless. Let me ask you a question, Jett, now that you have been introduced to a larger cosmic perspective."

"Sure, Chi-Col. Shoot."

"What percentage of life in what you call the Milky Way, do you believe all life on Earth represents?"

"A couple of weeks ago, I would have said 100%. Now, I'm going to guess significantly less than that."

"Let's agree it is a very small number, and your species is an infinitesimal fraction of that number."

"So then why are we such a threat to The Fold?"

"You are no threat to The Fold, but you are a threat to many other civilizations on their own winding roads to peace and happiness or wherever their free-will takes them," Chi-Col stopped, "We have arrived at The Garden."

A door appeared in the featureless wall before them and opened into a verdant garden. Jett was escorted into the bright sunshine of the sprawling Council Garden complex with its thousands of amphitheater seats. Unlike Jett's last visit, this time the seats were already filled and ushers waited at their stations. The Council was assembled and they were waiting for Jett.

"Great, they're probably already reading my thoughts."

"You can count on it, Jett," Nomika responded, "but I will help you to calm your mind before you are seated before Them. Please sit down, I will join my mind with yours and take you into a deep hypnosis. Your mind will feel no stress in this heightened state and your thoughts will integrate better with those of The Council."

Chi-Col and Nomika guided Jett to a chair that grew out of the ground. As Jett got closer, he noticed the chair was a large flower. Against his better judgment, Jett sat down inside it. The flower's fragrance intoxicated Jett. He became very drowsy. Fingertips caressed each of his temples.

"It is Nomika. Do not be afraid. Breathe deeply the deji flower's pollen. It will melt your troubles..."

Jett felt himself floating up and out of his body. He looked down at his unconscious self. Was he dead or was he dreaming?

"You are not dreaming, Jett, and you are most certainly not dead. You are, for lack of a better description, in a state of higher consciousness."

Jett looked up and saw Dr. VaaCaam-a.

"Please allow me to welcome you once again to The Garden. Do you know why you've been brought back here?"

"I am to ask The Council's forgiveness and beg it to spare my planet the fate of Boona and so many other systems?" Jett answered uncertain.

"No, that is not why, but it is the answer I expected you to share with us. The reason you were brought here is so you may understand the challenge your planet poses for us as we weigh its fate."

"So you haven't decided to neutralize Earth, um Solaris 3?"

"No we have not. Fortunately, none among your species has been able to replicate your Quantum Swapper. Until they do, there is no need to punish them."

"So you admit that neutralizing Earth would punish and potentially murder billions of innocent people. Isn't this a violation of The Ten Laws?"

"Before I answer that question, I would like you to understand that murder of any kind is deplorable regardless of the circumstances under which it is committed. The Fold never *murders* anyone or anything. Reliance on technology for sustaining life force is the real killer."

"Yes, but you are the ones flipping the switch off."

"Let me ask you a question, Jett. What do you think would happen on Aaptuu 4 if it was suddenly neutralized by a race even more advanced than our own? Before you answer you need to know that such races do exist throughout our Universe."

"Umm, nothing?"

"Not nothing, but not a single Aaptuuan would go hungry or want for anything. None would perish in resource wars. Our society is sustainable *without* any artificial power source. Every plant you see is edible, every insect useful, everything renewable. This is not true of your planet. This is why you worry so much about someone 'flipping the switch off'," Dr. VaaCaam-a continued, "Your civilization is *not sustainable without artificial supports*. Your species consumes without bounds. Your planet is sick and it is getter sicker with every moment that passes. You believe you are so very far

189

from the viruses and bacterium you seek to destroy, but you are no different. You are driven by the same insatiable hunger to consume and multiply. This hunger is limited only by the constraints of the resources available to you. Solaris 3 is sick, and your species is the disease."

Dr. VaaCaam-a paused and waited for Jett's reaction, but Jett's mind was quiet and receptive.

"Your species, you, have managed to create a device that has the potential to spread that disease throughout the cosmos, and yet you compare our decisions to a violation of The Ten Laws. The Fold sees it quite differently. For us, the neutralization protocol is antibiotics."

This comparison caused Jett's relaxed body to perk up, "So we are nothing more than bacteria to The Fold?"

"You misunderstand me," Dr. VaaCaam-a corrected, "you are much more than mere bacteria. The problem is that your species tends to treat all other species you draw under your dominion no better than bacteria, yet you conduct yourselves in so similar a manner to those simple creatures. This alone would not be a concern if your species were contained to one planet or one system. It becomes an urgent consideration when your species suddenly possesses the ability to move about the galaxy at will. Do you know of the dinosaurs?"

"Of course," Jett answered.

"Your scientists consider dinosaurs to be extinct, but they are not. They adapted. Dinosaurs survived upheaval by taking to the air. They became birds. Humans, too, face an evolutionary hurdle and you will overcome it by taking to the stars.

"You worry that neutralization might render the human race extinct, but consider this. The human race currently faces a 92.746% chance of significant population correction and a 68.241% chance of total extinction within the next seventy-five years if it stays on its current course. Neutralization would raise the risk of significant population correction to 100% in the immediate term, but lower the chances of total extinction to a much more palatable 14.66%."

"How do you know this?" Jett asked.

"You know how we know, Jett. You saw it for yourself on Boona."

"So we're more doomed if you leave us alone?"

"Mathematically, yes, but worry not, life on Solaris 3 will continue on."

"How do we change?"

"Now that is the right question. Today your species is seduced by the power of willful ignorance. You freely foul your air and water - the very things that sustain life. You kill each other en mass in the name of creed, nationality, and ethnicity. You divert massive nutritional resources to animals that you slaughter by the billions while your huddling masses die of starvation. These acts are committed with untold apathy and systematic cruelty. And while there is good in your species, it manifests itself against a stacked deck.

"You ask, 'how do we change' and I might simply tell you - follow The Ten Laws, but we both know that that has not worked out for you so far. Instead of telling you what you must do, I will tell you instead what you must forsake. If your species is to survive, thrive, and eventually gain admittance into The Fold, it must forsake the evils which plague it. These are:

Fear - because it denies all that is good.

Greed - for the possession of material things above all else is an affront to The Great White Light.

Anger - as those who live with rage can never know love.

Intolerance - which closes the mind to righteousness.

Deceit - which ultimately deceives the deceiver.

Jealousy and Envy - because they rob you of happiness for others and their achievements.

Cruelty - which attracts all the other evils as a magnet attracts iron filings.

Mercilessness - as it steals joy and harmony and hardens the heart.

There are more evils I could list, but if Solarians turned their backs on these, the others would shrivel in the wake of LOVE, JOY, and LIGHT. Love rules the Cosmos. If only your species could embrace the good, the positive, and harness the power that lies latent in the fabric of the Universe. It is right there before you, and yet you do not see it through the fear and anger. You constantly tear down that which you seek to build. You enslave yourselves to an artificial devil of your own making.

The Fold has documented every aspect of your species evolution over the last 30,000 Solarian years. From time to time, we have done our part to influence your evolution from the periphery with the hope that you would exercise your freewill for the mutual benefit of all."

"But we haven't done this, have we?"

"No you haven't. You've ignored The Ten Laws and today your planet pays the price. You need look no further than Solaris 2 to see what the future holds for Earth should you continue to pursue your current course."

"You mean, Venus?"

"Yes, Venus. Run away global warming, resource wars, mass extinction. Neutralization is a gift. You are not emotionally evolved enough to accept this fact."

"I'm beginning to understand it..."

"Still you do not accept it."

"I cannot accept it. Life as I know it would cease to exist."

"Indeed it would, and it must, but life would continue to flourish. Your species, like the Boonans, would see neutralization as a punishment. At first you would see yourselves as victims, but in time you would come to understand the gift we offer."

"The gift? Why not offer us your technology so we may avoid such a fate?"

"You are not ready. There is not enough love. There is not enough compassion. There is not enough empathy. You are selfish. Our technology would benefit the few where it is intended for all. You are not so different from us, and yet you are not so different from the dinosaurs. You possess a highly developed neo cortex adrift in a sea of limbic brain impulses. Our hope is that you, Jett, are able to work with us to convince your species to free themselves of negative thoughts and adopt the way of The Ten Laws."

"Why do you think anyone will listen to me?"

"It is our hope that through you, our message can be heard."

"Others have brought your message to humanity. Why

will they listen to me?"

"They are already listening."

"What?"

"They are already listening. The cat, as you say, is out of the bag."

Chapter 25
Bunnies- A Plague Upon the Earth

"So essentially you're telling me that kid 'beamed' into my office?" President Montoya asked, "like on Star Trek?"

"That's correct, Mr. President. We've reviewed all of the video footage. There's no other explanation."

"And now he's vanished along with that machine of his?" The President pressed.

"Taken by two grays, best we can tell," a scientist wearing a lab coat with a large hole in the sleeve offered.

"Your lab coat, Mr. Bannister?" The President asked pointing at his exposed arm. He looked at the others and examined their clothing.

"And you, Agent Smith, where's your pant leg? Patel?"

Jay Patel, who had turned his back to the meeting to get himself a glass of water, looked over his shoulder and responded confused, "Excuse, me sir?"

"Your suit, Jay. What happened to it? It's in tatters."

Jay looked into a large mirror that hung on the wall opposite him and saw that what remained of his pants hung from his belt in long thin strips. He stammered, "I don't understand, sir, though it does explain why it feels so cold in here."

"Get some clothes on, Patel."

"Yes, sir, but I, don't…" Jay stammered as he hurried out of the Situation Room.

"Where are my shoe laces?" an agent off in the corner asked.

"Mine are missing, too," another agent chipped in.

"What is going on with you people? I need you to hold it together. A fourteen year old boy somehow 'beamed' into my office and a short time later was abducted by aliens! I need answers!"

"Sir, look," Agent Smith pointed to the sink.

"What is that," Dr. Bannister asked curiously.

"They're red balls, like the one that boy had with him, only much smaller," Agent Smith reported running to the bar, "There must be dozens of them, and they seem to eat fabric," Agent Smith said pointing to two small red balls working their way up his remaining pant leg."

Two agents rushed into the Executive conference room. The first one said, "Mr. President, we have a problem. The red balls are overrunning the White House."

"What do you mean, *overrunning?*" Montoya responded.

"Sir," the second agent interjected, "They are pouring out of the plumbing all over The White House!"

"Can't you catch them?"

"We are trying sir, but we need heavy rubber gloves as they tend to spray acidic slime if we handle them roughly."

"Then try being nicer!" Agent Smith said as he gently plucked the two bush bunnies off of his pant leg and held them in his hands, "they're actually kinda cute."

"Kind of cute, Agent Smith?" The President snarled angrily, "I want them contained now! Lock down this facility. We can't afford to have an outbreak."

"They're fine if you're gentle. Round them up, but be careful not to startle them. The two that I'm holding here are, well, purring, I think. Put out piles of paper, clothing, and whatever else you think will attract them. Then gently pluck them off the piles and place them in boxes filled with stuff they eat. Whatever you do, keep them calm! Store them all in examination Room 6, it has an independent air handling system. I'll be there shortly with further orders," Agent Smith said.

"Yes, sir," the two agents replied in unison and raced off.

"I need everyone here to follow Mr. Smith's example. Carefully pick up any little fluff balls in your immediate vicinity and carry them to Room 6. I want the Executive Conference room cleared and I need everyone back in here in ten minutes," President Montoya ordered.

The President's cabinet went to work collecting the bush bunnies. They were careful not to startle any. As they filled their arms with the little creatures, the bunnies contently ate their jackets, shirts, ties, and other clothing, so that by the time the bunnies were deposited in room 6, their captors were left a ragged bunch. Yet bush bunnies continued to pour out of the drains and vents at a rate far in excess of the staff's ability to corral them.

President Montoya was himself down to little more than the remnants of a white oxford shirt, tattered pants, and half a tie.

"Mr. President, I have NATO leaders ready for you by video conference as you requested," a voice announced over the intercom.

"Good, put them through," a disheveled and nearly naked President Montoya responded.

"Coming through now, sir."

The large monitor opposite The President's black leather chair lit up with twenty-seven equal sized squares in three rows. President Montoya looked up and addressed the alliance.

"Fellow NATO member countries, thank you for making yourself available on such short notice. I have called you together to discuss a matter of urgent international security."

"Excuse me, Mr. President. Are you quite alright? You and your staff appear to be rather scantily dressed for such an urgent security matter," U.K. Prime Minister Sotheby interrupted.

"Yes, Prime Minister, we are ok. We are dealing with a little bit of an infestation at the moment."

"An infestation of what?" Sotheby pressed.

"An infestation of these," President Montoya said as he held up a half dozen ping pong sized bush bunnies in his hands.

"What are those?" President Le Fleur of France asked curiously.

"We don't know. We suspect they may be from another solar system. They are multiplying at an astonishing rate and appear to eat plant based materials. Fortunately for us, they aren't carnivorous, but regardless, they are literally eating us out of house and home. Have any of you had recent encounters with grays?"

The NATO members all agreed that they had not.

"Well, two of them visited The White House not an hour ago and abducted a young boy we had in custody."

An agent burst into the Executive Conference room, "Sir, you're needed on the Observation Deck!"

"NATO allies, please be on the lookout for any alien

activity. We will reconvene at 15:30. That is all," he finished and the video screen went black. The President ran out into the hallway. Nearly everyone he saw was down to little more than their shoes, underwear, belts, and gun holsters. Bush bunnies rolled up and down the hallways with impunity.

"I want these creatures contained!" the President demanded.

"Sir, we are trying our best, but there are too many," the agent responded.

President Montoya hurried into the Observation Deck. On the monitors he could see that the creatures had infested most of The White House and some had even made their way outside to the Rose Garden.

"Get Area 51 on the phone immediately!"

"Coming through now, sir," a tattered communications officer replied.

"Mr. President, we've received word that you've been visited by two grays and that now you may have alien life roaming The White House," General Donner said, "How can we assist?"

"We are transmitting the video of the grays abducting the boy, Jett, from a secure area. They teleported their way into the laboratory. I need your team to confirm whether these grays match the cadavers from the Roswell crash. Alert me immediately once you've completed your analysis. I need you to make this your top priority."

"Yes, Mr. President," General Donner confirmed.

"Assemble the Joint Chiefs. We are at DEFCON 3. Agent Smith, find out all you can about this Jett Javelin. I want to know where he lives, who his family is, who he hangs out with, where he was before he showed up here, and how he made that teleporter."

"Right away, sir."

The Observation Deck's pace immediately escalated from frenetic to frantic. Bush bunnies spilled out of the filing cabinets, covered control panels, and gorged themselves on paper folders, envelopes, and reams of copy paper. They chewed on the door frames and wooden chair legs. Montoya looked up to see bush bunnies consuming an original painting of George Washington.

"I don't believe our insurance will cover this," he mumbled.

"Mr. President, you need to see this!" the communications officer shouted.

President Montoya turned his attention to the big monitor. The video of Jett's abduction along with those of the bush bunny outbreak were being aired on CNN and Fox news.

"Oh my God," Montoya gasped, "assemble the press corps. We need to go into damage control. Find out who leaked these!"

The President stared at the video monitors. Within minutes, news of "White House Alien Abduction" and "Bush Bunny Outbreak!" was breaking on ABC, CBS, NBC, and all of the cable news outlets.

"The whole idea of it seems preposterous!" one commentator declared.

"No telling with special effects these days," another challenged.

"The end of times?" a third offered.

"There's no proof that there aren't aliens," an

interviewee pondered.

President Montoya closed his eyes. Pandora's Box was cast wide open and out of it spilled an alien apocalypse.

Chapter 26
Comparing Notes

"We've already told you everything we know," Evelyn pleaded, exhausted.

"Mrs. Javelin, this is a matter of national security," Agent Smith emphasized, "We have reason to believe that an alien race is holding your son for purposes yet unknown. Further, we believe those ETs may be planning an offensive against Earth in the near term. You've seen the videos on the news?"

Evelyn nodded that she had.

"It's imperative that we know everything your son told you. You say that Jett's invention is based on several of your quantum entanglement papers. Where are those kept?" Agent Smith asked.

"They're at my lab. I can have my assistant provide you with copies."

"Agent Williams, get over to her lab and collect those papers immediately."

"Yes, sir."

"Mrs. Javelin, you mentioned that your son Jett warned you about something called The Fold and their Ten Laws. What exactly did he say was going to happen?"

"He told us that if humanity doesn't wake up, Earth will be neutralized," Jett Sr. offered, "He said that The Fold would essentially turn off the lights, that electronic devices would be rendered useless, but there still was a chance they'd change their minds if we began following The Ten Laws."

"He also said that his invention is why they want to

neutralize us," Jack offered.

"Jack!" Evelyn scolded.

"Tell us more about that, Jack," Agent Smith pressed.

Jack looked at his mom, and she nodded that it was ok, so he proceeded, "Jett's invention allows him to travel between two locations in space no matter the distance. After he showed it to Ravi and me up in his room, he disappeared for a couple months. Then he suddenly turned up the day before yesterday butt naked with a little fuzzy ball from another planet."

"Yes, we are familiar with Nukii," Agent Smith said introspectively, "Tell me about Ravi."

"Ravi is Jett's best friend. He lives a couple blocks from here."

The doorbell rang. Jett Sr. excused himself to answer it. Upon opening the door, he was confronted by a dozen microphone bearing reporters and their video crews.

"Mr. Javelin, tell us about your son, Jett. Where is he right now?" the first reporter asked.

"Is it true that your son was abducted by aliens who are, at this very moment, bent on the destruction of Earth?" a second interrupted.

"Well, I, um," Jett Sr. stammered.

Agent Smith rushed to the door, "This interview is over. The Javelins are in protective custody and you are trespassing on private property," Agent Smith motioned to his fellow agents to escort the reporters away from the house.

Smith turned to the Javelin family and warned, "You're not safe here. We need to get you to a secure facility. We're leaving immediately."

"We know our rights," Evelyn interrupted, "We're not going anywhere."

"With all due respect, Mrs. Javelin, your lives are in danger. There are many who blame your son for bringing about the end of times. Now that the press has figured out who he is and where he lives, you and your family are in real danger."

A large rock crashed through the living room window sending shards of glass flying through the air. Scribbled on it in black sharpie were the words: 'Rot in Hell!!!'

"Mrs. Javelin, I believe this message and the manner in which it was delivered underscores the urgency of the situation. You are not safe here. I will leave several of my colleagues behind to protect your property. Right now, your safety is my primary concern."

"I thought your primary concern was interrogating me about my son," Evelyn shot back.

"Please, Mrs. Javelin. If what your son says is true we have very little time to argue. To be honest, I wouldn't have believed any part of this wild story if I hadn't seen the aliens myself."

"Wow, Jett was telling the truth," Jack reflected.

"Son, we're still unraveling the truth," Smith remarked.

"Honey, what do you want to do?" Jett Sr. asked Evelyn.

"Ok, let's go. I mean, if we can help...," she answered softly.

"Bring the cars around," Agent Smith ordered into his headset, "Folks, please come with me."

Agent Smith looked out the window at the gaggle of reporters gathered on the sidewalk across the street. They were now joined by a group of protesters holding signs that ran the gamut:

THANKS JETT YOU JERK!

OUR LORD DOTH COMETH

JESUS IS LORD

JUDGMENT DAY IS UPON US

BEAM ME UP, JETTIE!

Three large black SUVs pulled up in front of the house.

"It's time. Let's go. Please follow me closely and stay together," Smith directed.

He opened the front door and shouted, "Move! Now!"

The Javelins followed Smith down the red brick walkway to the waiting SUVs. The protesters booed, yelled, and cheered at them as they went. The reporters rushed forward shouting questions:

"Have you heard from Jett?"

"How much time does Earth have left?"

"What are those fuzzy red balls?"

The motorcade sped off through the neighborhood. An unfazed Smith continued right where he left off, "So, Jack, you were telling me about Ravi..."

Chapter 27
The Folly of Our Way

"Breaking news, we are not alone in the Universe. Mysterious videos leaked from the White House show a young boy being abducted by supposed extraterrestrial beings. Jett Javelin Junior of San Jose, CA is rumored to be the boy in the video. We are broadcasting live from outside his family's home on Tappliane Drive and it's a mob scene out here, Jim and Barbara. As you can see, to my right a group with peace banners and candles hold a nighttime vigil while to my left protesters shout 'end of world' slogans. The police presence here is intense. Officers in riot gear have set up a barrier between the two groups and tonight keep an uneasy peace.

"The Javelin family has been shuttled away by government agents and their home remains under the guard of the Secret Service and local police. Reporting from San Jose, CA this is Dan Howard, CNN News. Jim and Barbara back to you."

"Thanks, Dan. Have you interviewed anyone at the scene and if so what are they saying about Jett Javelin?" Barbara asked.

"Feelings were mixed as I worked my way through the crowd, here's what some of them had to say:

"I can't wait for our alien masters to arrive. Ol' Barney here and I have been preparing for years," said an old woman holding up her fat orange cat.

"BLEEP that stupid kid and his BLEEP BLEEP family, and invention, and bringing all hell and BLEEP BLEEP BLEEEEEEP down upon us. BLEEP it all!"

"I think this kid Jett is a hero and should be recognized

for putting us on the galactic road map. It's about time someone did."

"The name's Herbert Neninjer, and I don't care 'bout none of this alien stuff so shut yer yapper already!"

"Are there really little fuzzy red balls in the White House? Do you know where my mommy can buy me one?" a little girl with curly brown hair asked meekly, "I think they're really cute."

"As you can see, opinions are mixed, and yes, what about those fuzzy red balls?"

"Does anyone there know anything about the red balls, Dan?" Jim asked.

"I'm afraid not, but rumors of the fuzzy red balls and witnesses claiming to have seen and handled them are everywhere."

"Thanks, Dan. Be safe out there," Barbara said.

"Yes, I will."

"Thanks, Dan," Jim followed up and Dan's image faded, "Everyone is wondering - What are those fuzzy red balls? Are they the aliens' infant offspring; a cute and fuzzy gift from a soon to arrive alien race; or a plague of epic proportions?"

"That's right, Jim. Video footage coming out of the White House compound shows scantily clad agents, staffers, and workers rushing about. Insiders tell us that the creatures eat plant based materials including: cotton, wool, polyester, wood and paper products, and even human hair. President Montoya himself is rumored to be holed up in the Situation Room in nothing but a t-shirt and briefs. The videos have gone viral."

"Let's take a look at some of those videos now," Jim

said.

The video rolled. It showed a nearly naked White House staff filling up rooms with fuzzy red balls or chasing them up and down hallways. Scantily clad soldiers wearing little but helmets and machine guns stood guard. The video goes to black as several fuzzy red balls roll over the lens and presumably consume the camera.

"Oh my goodness," Barbara gasped, "Could this be some elaborate hoax?"

"That's what we're all wondering, Barbara. Is this real or just a hoax? Stay tuned for more about Alien Invasion 2028 after these words from our sponsors."

"Great!" President Montoya yelled as he slammed his television remote on the conference table, "Now the world knows I'm in my underwear! How did these videos get out? I want those responsible for the leaks brought in here immediately! Lock everything down! We can't afford any more leaks or this thing is going to get out of control. What's the status of the Javelin family?"

"They are being held at Vandenberg. We have the mother's research papers. Copies have been sent to Los Alamos."

"What have we learned?"

"Apparently, Jett told his family a more detailed version of the story he told us."

"Go on," President Montoya pressed.

"His invention is the reason the aliens, he called them Aaptuuans, are targeting Earth. He told them that The Fold is of the opinion that humans can't be trusted with technology of this nature and that we must be contained."

208

"Well, can you blame them?" the President asked as he motioned to monitors displaying riots and looting, "The rumors alone have half the planet on tilt. So what's going to happen next?"

"We're not sure. The Javelins don't appear to have any more insight than we do, except that it seems the correct thing to do now is to NOT create another teleportation device."

"Why not?"

"According to the Javelins, doing so would trigger a 'neutralization'."

"How do they know?"

"Jett told them that as long as the only working version of the device is off the planet, we're safe."

"Ok, so what do we do in the meantime?"

"You need to address the world. You need to calm their nerves. You must compel them to return to their lives. They need to know that everything will be ok."

"How can I convince them of that when I'm not so sure myself?"

"You must."

The President paused for a moment. He examined the screens. 'Alien Invasion 2028' - 'End of the World as We Know It?' - 'Judgment Day' - 'Panicked Crowds Flood the Streets of Los Angeles' - 'War of the Worlds Suicide Epidemic Revisited?' - And so on.

He considered the Javelin family's testimony. He understood The Ten Laws well as he had been exposed to an eerily similar set of commandments his whole life. Had this alien race been monitoring the Earth since biblical times or longer? Had they first introduced our species to the Ten

Commandments? The idea was both fantastic and unimaginable.

"Perhaps", he mumbled, "these beings were mistaken for gods over the millennia. Or is it possible they worship the same god and act as his galactic messengers? In either case, our best hope is to gain their favor and push for peace. We must feed the hungry. We must forgive past transgressions. We must lay down our arms."

And as The President gently stroked a softball sized bush bunny, he considered the case for peace, and saw the wisdom in it. It was time for the human race to wake up; wake up to a larger consciousness; A wider universe. He would not allow fear of the unknown to cloud his judgment.

"Let's face it" he said, "a disjointed, uncoordinated, low tech military response to the aliens' arrival would be akin to hornets defending their nest against an exterminator in a bee suit. If this race has been studying the Earth for thousands of years, they could have wiped us out long ago. They're obviously not interested in conquest, and it's unlikely they'll eat us," he trailed off in thought.

All things considered, the world was in pretty rough shape. Endless military skirmishes raged on against a backdrop of extreme weather, income inequality, resource shortages, and super bugs. These creatures could likely remedy all these problems and more if the human race proved worth their efforts.

The Earth stood no chance in a fire fight. His only option was to make it known to the people of Earth and extraterrestrials alike that peace was the only path forward. The United States would lay down its arms.

"I will address the world. Inform the press corps."

Chapter 28
Damned If I Do

Jett stood bravely before the Aaptuuan council.

Dr. VaaCaam-a telepathed to the room, "Based on the evidence, can anyone see any reason why this species should not be neutralized?"

Jett immediately stood up and said "My planet may not be perfect, but we don't deserve to have our power switched off just because of one invention! You say that taking away our electricity might save humanity but it would kill billions in the process. Meanwhile The Fold possesses the technology to help us."

"I propose neutralization for the whole system," said an Aaptuuan named Theadsrat, "the boy and his species pose a grave threat to peace and the evolution of other societies. Even now they loot and savagely kill each other at the prospect of our arrival," he concluded as a 3D hologram of mayhem and burning buildings appeared in the center of the amphitheater.

"This is true," Dr. VaaCaam-a agreed thoughtfully, "And do not forget that the Solarian leaders have done very little to end it non-violently."

"You have got to be kidding me!" Jett moaned, "All you need to do is lend us some of your tech, take my quantum swapper, and destroy all copies of the blue prints!" He continued, obviously annoyed, "If you do these three things we're no longer a threat, right? If you like, you can even give the people of Earth, sorry, Solaris 3 a primer on the importance of following The Ten Laws."

"While these options may seem reasonable to you,

they are irrelevant. You have shown humanity that teleportation is possible. Now many will attempt to replicate your feat. As we speak, scientists on Solaris 3 are pouring over your plans and assembling prototypes."

"How are my options irrelevant?" Jett asked, "You have the technology to usher in a new enlightened age for Earth."

"Our technology," Dr. VaaCaam-a replied, "is almost infinitely more wonderful than your species can appreciate. You would use it to enshrine a few in lavish opulence while the masses suffer in squalor and poverty. Our technology is a great equalizer. Overnight, it would put you on par with civilizations thousands of years more advanced. To put it plainly, you simply can't be trusted with it.

"We are sorry that your quantum exchanger has pushed humanity to an evolutionary crossroads. We do not wish to neutralize any civilization, but it is our duty to The Great White Light to maintain peace in this galaxy and beyond. Solarians are unique in many ways from others we have neutralized through the millennia," Dr. VaaCaam-a explained, "For example, one of your most interesting traits is your general level of disagreement with one another. For every cause there exists a faction, and for every faction a cause - good, bad, or indifferent. As a result, your species is far from possessing a unified consciousness. This is deeply concerning to us."

"Okay, so The Great White Light is guilt-tripping you into killing billions of people in the name of peace. Well, I have a big shocker for you, murder isn't peaceful!"

"We do not feel guilt as you understand it. The Great White Light demands peace, but your species is not ready for the kind of peace It demands. That peace requires your species to lay down all of its weapons, forsake monetary exchange, cease consumption of animals for food, and provide equally for all. There are a few among you who understand these requirements at a deep level: Gandhi, Martin Luther King Jr., Mother Teresa, Malala Yousafzai, Nelson Mandela, Albert Einstein, Leonardo Da'Vinci, Buddha, and Jesus Christ are some names you will recognize, but millions more toil in anonymity. They struggle against a system that is rigged by a powerful ruling class. The system is rotten and it gnaws at the collective consciousness of your species. Yours is a house divided against itself."

"So no help then?" Jett murmured.

"You are very upset right now, and we understand that, but sarcasm will do little to save Earth."

"Okay... sorry, it's just that having the fate of an entire planet on my shoulders is a little stressful." He paused, "How about this, you go to Earth and set up a peace keeping effort to ensure adoption of The Ten Laws. To start with, you can take everyone who has murdered another needlessly to some kind of holding center."

"So what you propose is that we come to Solaris 3 and remove all of the murderers. Then what?"

"Well, you could threaten to come back for the liars in a week, and the thieves after that, and so on until all who remain follow The Ten Laws."

"You propose coercion through the systematic removal of offending humans as a solution? We have studied your species' evolution for over 30,000 years. We are fairly certain that after a few short weeks there would be no one left on

Earth," a hushed laughter filled The Garden, "who among you hasn't lied to another or stolen something? In fact, by our strict definition of 'murder' only those who have been vegan from birth would qualify for your first exemption. Such a thing was once tried on Rocef 7 but the results were mixed."

"What do you mean 'mixed'?" Jett choked.

"Once the Rocefians learned of our existence, we intervened and attempted to guide their social evolution, but they were not ready. There was a brief period of peace followed by a violent civil war that lasted nearly two hundred years."

"What happened to them, the Rocefians, I mean?"

"Nearly eighty percent of the population perished in the aftermath of our intervention. The war was largely waged at the behest of a group known as The Front. They believed The Fold was bent on conquest and sought to set up a rigorous defense of their planet. Those who sought peace were wiped out. Military rule ensued. Today Rocef 7 is a post-apocalyptic world perched on the precipice. Are you prepared to send your species down the same perilous road?"

"I don't have a choice, do I?"

"Yes, you do."

"Well, then that is my choice, take the murderers away. If humanity isn't scared straight, then I'm afraid I've overestimated our intelligence and we deserve whatever we get."

"Are you sure, Jett? You cannot undo this once it is done."

"Yes, I'm sure," Jett replied swallowing hard, "At least the good among us will have a fighting chance. Neutralization favors the aggressive, my solution favors the meek."

"So it is decided. Let us begin with the murderers. Deploy a containment dome to Solaris 9."

Chapter 29
World Beyond Hope

"Mr. President, the world awaits."

"Isn't there anything proper for me to wear?" President Montoya asked.

"I'm afraid not, Sir. Those wretched creatures have eaten every article of clothing in The White House," a ragged Agent Smith replied, "You're going to have to go on air as is!"

Montoya turned and looked in the mirror. Were a Washington Nationals tank top and cargo shorts truly the best his staff could do for him? He looked ridiculous and weak. If he announced to the world that the United States was laying down all of its arms dressed like this, there was no telling how it would react.

"I look like a redneck on my way to a kegger. I can't go on the air looking like this."

"You must," Smith urged, "You have to instill calm," he continued pointing at monitor after monitor of looting and riots. "The world needs you and it needs you right now."

He took one last look at his reflection and smiled, "I suppose this outfit will get everyone's attention."

"Yes, sir."

"Ok, then. Let's do it," Montoya said confidently as he strode out onto the stage.

The press corps let out a collective gasp at the sight of The President.

Montoya did not allow this to shake him and he stood straight and tall as he grabbed the podium.

"Citizens of Earth," he began, "By now, most of you

217

have seen leaked video footage of strange, presumably extraterrestrial events occurring within the walls of The White House. Friends, I am here to tell you that the alien visitation, the abduction of Jett Javelin, and the subsequent infestation of this residence by red ball creatures from another planet are," he paused for a moment, gathered his resolve, and stared hard into the cameras, "unequivocally real."

The press corps erupted.

"Please, please, let me finish. There will be time for questions."

The room fell anxiously silent.

"We are not alone. In fact, we've never been alone. We now know that an advanced alien civilization has monitored us for most of human history. Moreover, we have reason to believe an alien contingent is, at this very moment, on route to Earth with the intention of delivering a message of peace.

"To honor their arrival and demonstrate our cooperative nature, I have issued an executive order requiring the United States armed forces to stand down. I have grounded all military and civilian flights and I have ordered a flight ban over all U.S. states and territories.

"I encourage friends, allies, and enemies alike to follow our example. To do so will demonstrate the solidarity of our planet.

"Many of you may be wondering why I am delivering such a message dressed this way. Those fuzzy red balls you've undoubtedly seen in the media have a ravenous appetite for clothing, paper, wool, hair, and just about any other inert organic material.

"If you encounter one of these creatures, please call

The White House hotline number displayed on your screen. The good news is that these creatures are not dangerous, I repeat they are not dangerous, but it is urgent that we contain them.

"I will now take questions."

"Mr. President, don't you feel that lowering our defenses opens us up to unreasonable risk?" a reporter shouted from the crowd.

"Actually, the Joint Chiefs and I feel differently. We know that this advanced civilization possesses the ability to switch our power off. Without electricity we are defenseless."

"Mr. President," a second reporter shouted, "How do we know these extraterrestrials are peaceful?"

"Well, Jim, we feel reasonably certain that if conquest was their intention, they would have done so centuries or even millennia ago. From what we know, The Fold, as it is called, is a federation of peaceful civilizations. Jett Javelin's discovery of matter teleportation makes the human race a threat to peace."

"If they are truly as advanced as you suggest then why would The Fold view us as a threat?"

"Take a look at Earth today. Civil wars and armed skirmishes rage in nearly every corner of our planet. We indiscriminately kill each other in ever increasing numbers over petty differences. Starvation and disease plague our planet as we continue to pollute it with reckless abandon. Jett's invention would allow us to export our aggression and insatiable material appetites anywhere in the universe. As President, if I were presented with a similar threat, I would seek to contain it at all costs."

"When do we expect representatives from The Fold to

arrive on Earth?"

"NASA tells me that several large unidentified craft have congregated in near Earth orbit. When they intend to make contact is unknown. I suspect they are listening to my address and I hope they see the actions of the United States and our allies as a positive step forward."

"What about our enemies? What if a rogue government or terrorist enterprise seized upon this opportunity to launch a large scale attack on U.S. interests?"

"Those entities will need to answer to The Fold."

The room filled with a static electric charge. President Montoya felt the hair on his arms stand up. There was a bright flash and Jett, Chi-Col, and Nomika joined Montoya at the podium.

The press corps jumped to its feet. The unannounced arrival of Jett and his two Aaptuuan keepers shocked the room and the world.

"Earth is not ready for the technology I invented. Humans, left unchecked, will become a galactic plague. Look no further than our own planet for proof of this. I am sorry that I did this to you, my fellow citizens of Earth, but I'm here to tell you that it is not too late to choose a different path.

"Earth must obey The Ten Laws as laid down by The Great White Light and enforced since time immemorial by The Fold. These laws are:

> Do not kill others
> Do not steal from others
> Do not lie to others
> Do not sow discord among others
> Do not feel envy for others' possessions

Do not act selfishly
Do not hold hatred in your heart
Honor your forebears
Honor your offspring
Love everything

"We have had thousands of years to reflect upon and follow the wisdom contained in these ten simple laws. Yet today, we act as though they do not exist and do not matter or that we may pick and choose those that serve our own selfish ends. Fortunately, for now, The Fold has agreed not to neutralize Earth. Instead it has chosen to send a very clear and concise message to the people of Earth - every human of adult age must, from this day forth, follow The Ten Laws to the letter.

"To drive this home, The Fold will soon remove all humans who have committed the atrocity of murder. These souls will be relocated to a rehabilitation facility on Solaris 9, or what we know as the dwarf planet, Pluto. The Fold's agents will return in the near future to collect the thieves, liars, and cons. Good behavior exhibited between now and their return will be taken into consideration.

"Your cooperation is strongly encouraged. As a reminder of the importance of your compliance, all broadcast, satellite, and web content will display one of The Ten Laws for each of the next ten days after which time, content control will be returned to human hands."

With that, Jett and the Aaptuuans vanished. The live feed from The White House and all global media outlets and websites changed to a simple black screen with white letters that read: *Do not kill others*. Radio stations broadcasted a soothing, yet authoritarian, voice that repeated *Do not kill others* over and over again. Slips of paper containing The Ten Laws rained down from the sky in every language over every city on Earth.

"Mr. President, we've lost control of the feeds."

"See what you can do to..." Montoya began before he was interrupted,

"Sir, we have a bigger problem," Agent Smith interjected.

"What is it, Smith?"

"The red ball creatures... They somehow got out of The White House complex and have begun overrunning the city. Sir, there doesn't appear to be any reasonable method of containment."

President Montoya took it all in. He stared at the dozens of video monitors lining the room. All displayed the first law - do not kill others. He took a deep breath.

"Judgment has come. Let us embrace peace and love for our fellow man. Begin the distribution of food and medicine to the hungry and sick. Begin the process of disarmament. Let us show these beings that we are not beyond redemption."

Chapter 30
The Inevitability of Tomorrow

"This is Dan Howard reporting live from outside The White House where President Montoya is preparing his 'State of the Globe' address. It's been ten days since rumors of alien contact, abduction, and infestation were confirmed by The President of The United States in his live address to the world. Today marks the first day of restored broadcast, satellite, cable, and internet communications. Images of The Ten Laws have disappeared, but many questions remain.

"Reports of mass disappearances reverberate across the globe. Entire cell blocks of prisoners have 'vanished into thin air' to quote New York governor Ryan Gunderson in a letter to The President. Strangely, the governor notes that several inmates on death row were left behind. These presumably innocent prisoners have been pardoned along with all non-violent offenders.

"Several world leaders are now rumored to be missing along with Bin Ali Johanson - the mastermind behind the so called 'Autonomous Auto Massacre' which killed over 280,000 people and destroyed large swaths of infrastructure when Bin Ali's team of hackers assumed remote control of hundreds of thousands of self-driving cars and turned them into weapons of mass destruction. Barbara and Jim, it appears The Fold is keeping its word.

"Here in Washington DC everyone's asking what, if anything, the authorities will do about the fuzzy red balls now overrunning The Beltway."

"Yes, Dan, what about those red balls? We understand

223

they're called Lanedaarian Bush Bunnies and are from the planet Lanedaar 3, a planet Jett Javelin is believed to have visited," news anchor Barbara asked.

"What we know about the Lanedaarian Bush Bunnies is that they eat just about every plant and plant based material they can find," Dan said holding up a large bush bunny. "As you can see, this one here is well fed and quite friendly. So far as we know, no one has been seriously injured by a bush bunny, but they have become quite a nuisance.

"Behind me, bush bunnies are rolling up and down the streets and sidewalks of Washington D.C. by the thousand. They have completely denuded the Rose Garden, The White House's lawns and trees, and the surrounding area. This little rascal here is nibbling my coat sleeve."

"Dan, hold on, we're getting word that The President is about to begin his address. We're going live to Camp David where President Montoya and his staff have taken up residence in the wake of the bush bunny epidemic."

"Good evening fellow citizens of Earth. There is much to say about the events of the last Ten Days. Each day highlighted a single law and offered us each a chance to reflect on our individual choices and the plight of our planet.

"Thousands of prisoners, armed militia, and members of known drug cartels and violent gangs have disappeared without a trace. While this is a blessing to the peaceful majority, key figures in the military and armed services are also missing.

"It appears from the nature of the disappearances that the reason why a man took another man's life is entirely irrelevant. That a man took a life at all is enough.

"But there is hope. Over the last ten days reports of looting and incidents of violent crime have dropped to nearly zero. It's obvious to this President that many of you have taken The Fold's warning seriously.

"The United States and its allies have laid down our weapons. We believe that today marks a turning point in human history. We believe that today The Fold will deliver its tenth law - Love Everything.

"We encourage you to join us in our efforts to put a peaceful face on a violent world. Your actions today forth may not be judged solely by your fellow man, by your day in court, or by society. They will be judged by the very same authority that has 'disappeared' at last count, over 2,000,000 people in the U.S. alone.

"We must stand together in peace if we are to prove our worthiness. The age old saying 'The meek shall inherit the Earth' has never rung so true as it does today. Questions?"

President Montoya paused, "Yes, Bill."

"The grounding of air traffic has crippled the economy. When does your administration plan to end the flight ban?"

"Well, that's impossible to say. Obviously, we'd like to lift the ban immediately, but we feel the danger to the general public is too great."

"What is the danger of air travel?"

"Our intelligence informs us that if The Fold deems our species too violent, too barbaric, it will neutralize, or turn off, all electronics. Should this occur, planes would literally rain down from the sky. We will reestablish air travel once we are convinced it is safe to do so. Another question. Yes, Charlotte."

"What about..."

The transmission was interrupted. Jett's face filled screens across the globe.

"Fellow citizens of Earth. I have been asked to tell you that by this time tomorrow, every human that has taken another human's life will have been extracted from this planet and relocated to the First Law processing center on Solaris 9, um, I mean Pluto.

"I can tell you with all certainty that The Fold knows when you're sleeping and knows when you're awake, knows when you've been bad or good, so, well you know the rest.

"President Montoya is a wise man. His actions and those of his allies have bought much goodwill in the eyes of The Fold. As a result, Earth will not be neutralized at this time. It is safe to resume commerce by air, sea, and rail.

"While I regret that my invention has brought The Fold's judgment upon our humble little planet, I can't help but to wonder what the fate of Earth would have been without their intervention. Today, we clog the oceans with plastic and toxic waste; we crowd out all other species, and we kill each other by the million.

"I have traveled the galaxy and now recognize that we are a very, very insignificant little species trapped in a galactic backwater, looking for meaning, seeking purpose. Our civilization is but one of millions scattered among billions of stars.

"I know that this is very hard for many of you to understand, but the time has come for us to grow up and assume our place in galactic society. This can only happen if we choose the path of peace and love.

"Abandon hate, envy, jealousy, greed, and lust and

embrace love and kindness. Lift each other up for love is the only path to righteousness."

With these final words Jett turned away from the camera and walked across a lush open field. His image faded and was replaced by that of the tenth law - Love Everything.

By and by, Jett came to a row of simple military style homes lined up in tidy rows. Jett stopped in front of one particular house, turned, and walked up the narrow pavers to the front door. He knocked on the door, and his mother answered it.

"Oh, my baby!" she cried as she bent down to embrace him, "Honey, everyone, Jett's here!"

Jack and Jett Sr. rushed outside and took part in a large group hug. Stanford trotted up to Jett, tail wagging wildly, and licked his hands and arms. Nukii purred happily.

"It's good to have you back, Jett" his father beamed.

"Yeah, we missed you buddy, even if you almost destroyed the world," Jack teased.

"Jack, that's enough!" Evelyn said sternly, "Jett's been through enough without sass from you."

"It's ok, mom," Jett interjected, "It's just good to be here with you all."

Stanford barked wildly.

"What's wrong with Stanford?" Jett asked.

"Probably just excited to see you," Evelyn smiled, "We all are."

"Well, you're just in time. We were about to sit down to supper and it just so happens, we're having..." Jett Senior began, but vanished in a flash of light before he could finish his sentence. Stanford went berserk.

"Dad?" Jett gulped.

"What happened to him?" Jack asked, "What happened to dad?"

"Where did he go, Jett? Where did they take him?" Evelyn cried.

"Why would they take him? He's never killed anyone... has he?"

Evelyn stopped and stared blankly into space.

"Mom, dad never killed anyone right?" Jett pursued.

"Well, um..."

"Um, what, mom?" Jett continued.

"Both of you know that your father served in Afghanistan when he was younger."

"Yeah, but he was a base psychologist," Jack said dismissively, "They don't see any action."

"He did. His convoy was ambushed outside of Kabul. During the firefight, he shot and killed several militants."

"But that was in self-defense!" Jack declared, "That doesn't count as murder."

Jett looked down at his feet. What a cruel trick the Aaptuuans had played on him.

"Jett? What about self-defense?" Evelyn uttered.

Jett looked up stroking his father's dog tags. Tears welled up in the corners of his eyes, "The Aaptuuans don't see a difference. To kill is to kill, period."

"This is all your fault," Jack screamed, "You and your stupid invention!"

"Calm down, Jack," Evelyn ordered, "Jett, they'll send him back, right? I mean, once they find out he was acting out of self-defense in a war zone."

"I'm not sure," Jett replied dejectedly.

"Can't you ask them? You know them right?"

"Obviously not as well as I thought," Jett answered staring up into the sky. "And I have no way of contacting them now."

Jett collapsed to his knees.

Jett Sr. looked out at the night sky. Something wasn't right. One star looked much bigger and brighter than the rest.

"That's the sun," a tattooed man sitting nearby explained.

"The sun?" Jett Sr. replied incredulously, "but that's impossible. It's so small."

"Welcome to Pluto, friend. Who'd you kill?"

About the Authors

Evan Gordon is a middle school student who enjoys playing volleyball, reading novel after novel, acting in school plays, and watching Doctor Who.

Scott Gordon is President of HelioPower, an integrated energy services company, solar blogger, ukulele player, and public speaker who also happens to enjoy Doctor Who.

The pair are busily working away on the second book in the Problem With Solaris 3 series in between homework, business meetings, conference calls, Instagram, and, of course, episodes of Doctor Who.

They live in Orange County, CA.

Made in the USA
San Bernardino, CA
05 October 2015